Praise

"*Shadows among the Ruins* is a fast-paced and old-school fun mystery read, highly recommended."
—Midwest Book Review

"This 'who-done-it' has cops, a surprise ending, great dialog, and stunning vistas. This is the kind of book to dive into in front of a fire or to take on a plane and tune everything out."
—*Tradición Revista Magazine*

"Cash is an author who knows Santa Fe inside and out, from its Canyon Road art dealers selling million-dollar paintings to its drug-dealing bar scene and hard-working cops. She's not afraid to pile up the dead bodies and sling the slang around."
—Wolf Schneider, Reviewer for *New Mexico Magazine* and former Editor-in-Chief of the *Santa Fean*

"Marie Romero Cash writes about Santa Fe with a local's razor-sharp insights, and peoples her exciting mystery with a gallery of colorful, authentic New Mexico characters. The plot moves with the speed and force of a Southwestern thunderstorm."
—Kirk Ellis, Co-Executive Producer/Screenwriter, HBO's *John Adams*

"A gifted writer has entered the ranks of the best of Southwest Mystery Writers. From the first chapters I found myself caught up in the action, stifling a catch in my throat, actually hyperventilating. This book has the kick of a high-powered rifle."
—Tal Streeter, sculptor and author of many books, including *A Kite Journey through India*, *Art of the Japanese Kite*, and *Paper Wings Over Japan*

"*Shadows among the Ruins* is a great read whose real characters and honest dialog capture the intrigue of New Mexico. Throw in a great plot with a surprise ending, and mystery lovers will be clamoring for the sequel. Marie Romero Cash has taken the gift for prose she demonstrated in Lowrider Blues and applied it to the mystery genre with spectacular results."

—J. Michael Orenduff, Author, *The Pot Thief Murder Mystery Series*

"*Shadows among the Ruins* will compel some Southwestern mystery writers take another look at their own work. Marie Cash made me sit up and take notice. Her come-along plot made me miss dinner, but it was worth it. Now, after I get something to eat, I'm going to read it again. You have to like this book."

—Forrest Fenn, Santa Fe resident and owner of San Lazaro Pueblo, the setting for *Shadows*. He has written eight books on history, art, and archaeology.

"*Shadows among the Ruins* is a good read. Set in the American Southwest, the novel uses the landscape as a character. The author knows how to pace a mystery, how to develop suspense, how to build a backstory and she's not afraid of a little blood. This isn't a cozy, but a hard hitting, dynamic piece of writing. The killer, who shall remain unnamed, is a good adversary for the introspective sleuth, a lapsed Mormon called Jemimah. The novel is full of such surprises in the story line, in the characters and in the writing. I liked the epilogue in Brazil but won't spoil it for you. This sleuth in her landscape deserves a series. I hope the author brings her back for more death and mayhem. Buy it. Read it."

—Jack Remick, author of *Blood*, *The Deification*, and *Valley Boy*

DEADLY DECEPTION

A JEMIMAH HODGE MYSTERY

DEADLY DECEPTION

A JEMIMAH HODGE MYSTERY

MARIE ROMERO CASH

CAMEL
PRESS
Seattle, WA

Camel Press
PO Box 70515
Seattle, WA 98127

For more information go to: www.camelpress.com
www.marieromerocash.camelpress.com

Cover design by Sabrina Sun

DEADLY DECEPTION
Copyright © 2013 by Marie Romero Cash

ISBN: 978-1-60381-893-3 (Trade Paper)
ISBN: 978-1-60381-894-0 (eBook)

Library of Congress Control Number: 2012945320

Printed in the United States of America

**Other Books by Marie Romero Cash
in the Jemimah Hodge Mystery Series:**

Shadows among the Ruins

Coming Soon ...

Treasure among the Shadows

Prologue

On a side road running parallel to the Santa Fe Bypass, the winds stilled—as if by divine direction—and the rain dribbled to a stop. At that moment there was no wind, rain, or clouds.

It was late June, 2001. Shadows cast by the magnificent cottonwood in the middle of the field danced across the hood of the shiny red Corvette, its right front end bashed in from the crash. The impact had propelled the passenger from the vehicle, and now she lay in a crumpled heap on the sodden grass twenty feet away. Her head was bloody, her neck broken.

Don Ilfeld, moaning, had his fingers entwined around the steering wheel. He pushed on the door with his left shoulder. The pain was excruciating. He continued to brace himself on the dashboard for a few minutes to get his bearings. The temperature was eighty-seven degrees, but he was chilled to the bone.

The driver's side door flew open. He felt himself yanked upright and thrown against the tree.

"Ilfeld, you stupid son-of-a-bitch. You were supposed to hit the tree at an angle. No goddamned way she was going to be thrown that far. I had to drag her back another ten feet."

Don slid down the tree, wondering how he'd ever gotten himself into this mess. He tried not to look at the corpse of his wife, Rose.

⚘

One day earlier, Roger Streeter stepped onto the porch of a small adobe house on Santa Fe's posh east side, pressed the doorbell and waited. Rose Ilfeld was engrossed in her favorite pastime. Her hands caked with dirt, she tamped the fresh potting soil around the newly planted rose bushes. She sat at the center of a profusion of color, hundreds of plants bursting forth with blossoms. She was an attractive woman, with shoulder length wavy hair that framed an oval face. Her lime-colored tank top blended in with the greenery of the garden. She could easily have been the subject of a Monet painting.

"Back here, Roger," she hollered, wiping her brow with her sleeve.

Roger Streeter had known Rose Ilfeld for most of their lives. They had hit it off from the very first day the moving van had pulled in front of the house next door to his family's. They had remained good friends ever since.

Roger wound his way around the wheelbarrow and the dozen or so bags of potting soil and fertilizer spread across the pathway. "Hey, Rose. How's it going? I just came by to see how you're feeling. Don said you hadn't been well lately."

She was mystified as to why their best friend would think she had been ill. "Fine, Roger. Don's a worrywart."

"I guess. He said you were having a series of tests at the hospital. You sure you're all right?"

She rolled her eyes and laughed. "Well, duh. Would I be out here working in my garden if I was at death's door?"

"I'm confused," he pushed on. "How are your Leukemia treatments coming along?"

"Roger! Where would you get such an idea?" She stood and brushed the dirt from her apron.

"From Don. I must have misunderstood. Forget I mentioned it. He must have been talking about something else." Streeter was more perplexed than Rose was. From her reaction, he could see she had no idea what he was talking about.

"I guess so. The only condition I'm suffering from is insomnia, caused by my husband's relentless snoring."

"No matter. I was just on my way to work. Patti sends her regards."

"Sure you won't have a cup of coffee? I was just about to brew a fresh pot," she flashed the smile that captivated him the first time he'd seen her.

"'Fraid not. Just came by to say hi. Saw your car and figured you were home. Busy morning. I'll take a rain check."

"Well, give Patti my best," she reached out to hug him.

He bent down and kissed her forehead. "I will."

She waved him off and returned to the task of replanting the white hydrangeas. A burst of wind huffed into the yard, scattering plastic containers onto the walkway.

Roger Streeter was the first paramedic to arrive at the scene on the deserted stretch of Highway 85 on the outskirts of Santa Fe. The wail of sirens from a speeding ambulance broke the quiet afternoon. An old man in a beat-up truck pulling a trailer full of trash veered over to the shoulder to clear a path.

A State Police cruiser with lights whirling was already parked in the field. Streeter nosed the ambulance onto the grass as far as he could and jolted to a stop. The two EMTs jumped from the vehicle, slid the side doors open, grabbed their equipment and rushed forward to assess the injured. The red convertible lodged against the trunk of the massive Cottonwood looked vaguely familiar.

God, no, Roger thought. He knew that car.

His partner hurried to assess the man, propped against the cottonwood tree trunk. Blood dripped down his forehead. His features were distorted by bruising, but the man was obviously State Policeman Don Ilfeld.

Roger ran to the lifeless body of the woman. *Sweet Jesus, it was Rose.* She was lying so still. *Was she dead?* He took her limp wrist in his hand and checked for a pulse. *Nothing.* He tapped her head gently; her neck was broken. He was momentarily caught up in grief.

State Police Captain Jeff Whitney exited the black and white cruiser and walked over. "Hey, Streeter, when did you switch from Park Service to EMT?"

"Hey, Whit, I'm just trying out new career possibilities. Gotta do something after retirement." Streeter regained his composure. "Too many years out in the wilderness and 'fraid I'll miss it. You been here long?"

"Arrived a few minutes before you. Figured the woman was already dead. The guy's in pretty bad shape. Kind of out of it. A fellow police officer. That's his wife. Neither one was wearing seatbelts," Whitney droned on like they were strangers. "Head hit the windshield. I carried her out of the car just in case the damn thing decided to blow. Tried to resuscitate her. Didn't work."

Streeter couldn't see Whitney's eyes through the dark Ray-Bans. As usual, he was all business. Even though they'd been casual acquaintances for over twenty years, he knew Whitney's reputation as a hard ass. Just why the hell was he moving an injured person before the paramedics arrived? Streeter knew better than to ask.

"Yeah," said Streeter. "I know these people. Good friends of my family. She would never ride around without a seat belt." He leaned toward her body and gently touched the side of her head. She's got some bruising on her neck that doesn't jibe with being thrown through a windshield."

"Let the coroner make the assumptions, Streeter," Whitney said in an authoritative tone. "Transport Officer Ilfeld over to the ER. Don't want to lose both of them."

Santa Fe County Sheriff Jerry Purcell drove up and parked next to the police cruiser. Whitney walked over to the blue and silver four-by-four. "No use you getting out, Purcell. I've got it under control here. According to Officer Ilfeld, his wife passed out in their living room. He was taking her to the hospital, was in a hurry, lost control, skidded off the road, hit that tree. She's dead. He's a little worse for wear. We'll get him off to the hospital."

"Okay, if you say so. I got another call to tend." Purcell shifted his vehicle in reverse. It didn't matter whose jurisdiction this was, he'd let Whitney take care of it.

"Got a hot date?" Whitney asked.

Purcell waffled his hands, a shit-eating grin on his face. "Kinda, sorta. Let me know how everything turns out."

"Glad to accommodate you, Sheriff."

"Anyway, looks like he's out for the duration," Purcell added. The obvious bum's rush Whitney gave him didn't bother him a bit. He watched Whitney strut toward the medics, who were about to place Ilfeld on a stretcher.

"You two still hanging around here? Get a move on," said Whitney.

Streeter wanted to throw back Whit's observation about letting the coroner make the conclusions, but stifled the impulse. No point in angering the man. Unless he was prepared to make a stink that might cost him his job, he'd best keep his dark thoughts to himself. Maybe he was just too close to Rose to think clearly. It was easier to suspect that a death was suspicious than accept the random cruelty of fate, he supposed. She had been such a lovely woman.

Another State Police cruiser arrived, busted its way across the grass. Whitney signaled for him to park where the sheriff had just vacated.

Streeter's partner strapped an oxygen mask over Ilfeld's face. "Haven't been able to revive him. Might be in shock," he said.

Streeter lifted the man's eyelid and beamed a small flashlight into his eyes. "That's odd."

"What's odd?" the rookie tech asked.

"His pupils aren't dilated. Maybe he just passed out. Let's get him out of here before Captain Whitney gives us a citation for loitering. We'll have to leave the woman's body for the M.E." Streeter felt another wave of grief as he covered Rose's body with a sheet.

As they wheeled the gurney toward the ambulance, the front wheel hit a rock and almost catapulted the patient onto the ground. Ilfeld reached out to grab the metal sides of the gurney.

Streeter looked at the other medic. "In shock, my ass," he said under his breath. "More like the guy's faking."

Ilfeld moaned and closed his eyes, still holding on for dear life.

While Streeter loaded equipment and secured the back doors of the ambulance, he overheard Whitney talking to his fellow officer. "I'll make out the accident report. Guy in a hurry, missed the turn, spun out of control, skidded into a tree. Woman wasn't wearing a belt—Boom!"

Streeter spun rubber and the ambulance peeled out onto the highway. It was obvious there weren't any skid marks on the road. What sheep's eyes was Whitney trying to pull the wool over?

In the months that followed, he kept puzzling over the accident. Why would Ilfeld try to make his injuries look worse than they were? Why had Whitney been so eager to take the scene at face value? Why had Ilfeld spread rumors that his wife had a chronic disease? He tried several times to put a bug in the ear of someone who might at least consider the possibility that this had been no accident. But no one wanted to override Whitney. In the end, he let it go.

Chapter One

In the early months leading up to springtime, the weather in Santa Fe is as unpredictable as San Francisco fog. Gusty winds blow out of nowhere and howl until all hours of the morning. Bright sunshine can be replaced with dark clouds, followed by hail, sleet and snow all the way through May. But once the warm weather takes hold, temperatures can soar into the mid-nineties on any given day.

On Memorial Day in 2009, the season in Santa Fe was leaning toward summer, with unseasonably high temperatures. The weather in Cerrillos was different from Santa Fe's; the elevation of the small community nestled between Santa Fe and Albuquerque was a thousand feet lower, meaning that the air was warmer. Winters were less inclement, but that didn't preclude the occasional snow-dumping blizzard that went off course.

Lieutenant Detective Rick Romero was feeling the heat, not only from the weather but from the public. They were concerned about the recent surge of residential break-ins and vandalism. As Chief Detective, he was the one they looked to for answers.

Romero was lighter skinned than most of the native Hispanos in the area. He was in his early forties, five ten, and well-built, with dark hair and hazel eyes. Easily mistaken for Anglo, he fit into all the echelons of society.

He sat at his desk in the Cerrillos substation of the Santa Fe County Sheriff's Office. A few years back, Sheriff Bobby

Medrano had won a heavily contested election against incumbent Jerry Purcell. His first task had been to appoint Romero head of the new substation. Medrano was pleased with his overall performance and placed his name at the top of the list. In spite of a tendency to throw caution to the wind, Romero was a dedicated officer. It wasn't unusual for the Sheriff to reprimand him on a regular basis, but despite the many times he was called on the carpet, Romero was well liked and respected.

He reached for the phone on the third ring, dreading yet another complaint from a disgruntled Cerrillos resident about barking dogs, loud music, petty thievery and a slew of other minor occurrences.

"Sheriff's Office, Romero."

"Rick, Jemimah Hodge. How are you?"

He hadn't heard from Jemimah for more than six months. She had been on extended leave from her position as forensic psychologist with the Sheriff's Office to take an FBI forensics course in Washington, DC. She'd been the only person chosen from New Mexico, and one of the few women in attendance.

"Well, I'll be darned. A voice from the past," Romero said. "Finally decided to return home and make contact with your friends?"

"You don't really believe I'd give up my dog, my cat and my horses that easily, do you?"

"That's where I rank? Behind the pets and the horses." He leaned back in his chair and put his feet up on the desk. Damn, he had missed her. Of course he knew he wouldn't be sharing that particular thought.

"Well," Jem laughed. "I see you haven't changed much. Thought you'd mellow out in six months, maybe become a little less self-centered."

"Not when the gal I'm crazy about leaves without saying goodbye," he countered. "Oh, that's right. You did leave a

Post-it note on my office door. Let me see. What did it say? Oh, I remember. 'Bye. See you in six months.' "

"Rick, that's not fair. You know the opportunity came out of nowhere. I barely had time to pack my bags and arrange for the care of my animals."

"I know, I know. But you rubbed salt in an open wound, leaving like that. Didn't even get a chance to celebrate our success in solving the murders at San Lazaro Pueblo," he said. "Received the commendations all by myself. That sucked."

"Well, if it helps any, I am sorry. I hope it won't affect our working relationship."

He could hear the exasperation in her voice and knew he was pushing too hard, but he couldn't help himself. "I'm not sure about that. Particularly now that you have another title to add after your name," he pushed on, the hint of a pout in his voice.

"No title. Just another framed certificate to hang on my wall. So listen, as much as I'd like to sit around and chitchat down memory lane with you, I do need to set up an appointment to go over a few things."

"Sure, my schedule's pretty flexible."

"Sheriff Medrano handed me a cold case from 2001 and I'd like to discuss it with you."

So she was choosing to change the subject. Okay, he could go along with that. "What's it about, if I may ask?"

"In a capsule, a State Policeman's wife died in an accident about eight years ago. Coroner said her injuries were consistent with her head hitting the windshield. The family doesn't buy it, never bought it, and they keep exerting pressure on law enforcement to take another look. The EMT who first responded knew the woman and appears to have had his doubts as well."

Romero's tone of voice changed. "Oh, yeah. I remember something about it. Your friend Jeff Whitney was already a veteran state policeman at the time. He was the investigating officer. Maybe it's him you should invite to lunch."

There was a silence. Was that a sigh he heard? He could almost hear Jemimah counting to ten. Finally she said, "The problem with that idea is that this is the same cold case Whitney was supposed to review last year. He was the one who was told to turn in a full report to the Police Commission, who in turn would determine if it was worth reopening or not. Surely it hasn't slipped your mind that Whitney—"

"No, it hasn't slipped my mind, and you don't need to go into it anymore."

"Obviously, I do. You don't know everything, Romero. Whit and I met to discuss it last spring. Two months later he pulled back. I was in Colorado investigating the psycho girlfriend in the San Lazaro case. Whit never gave a reason for not filing a report—just called and said it wasn't worth pursuing."

"If memory serves, you two had an intimate luncheon at Los Angelos over margaritas and jalapeño poppers. So why's it coming round the pike again?" He almost gagged on his last swallow of coffee and spit it all over his desk. "Oops, sorry, down the wrong pipe."

"Hey, you need me to rush over and slap you with a Heineken maneuver?"

"A what?"

"Never mind. Nonetheless, your friend the State Police chief is being pressured by a State Senator—"

"Where does that leave pretty-boy Whitney?" Romero couldn't help himself. Whitney had thrown a monkey wrench in the works right about the time he became serious about dating Jemimah, and that wasn't a slight he intended to overlook.

Another pause. "Look, Rick," Jemimah said, her voice more clipped than ever. "This is official business. If you don't want to help, I'll ask the Chief to find me someone who won't pull this petty crap. Do you keep notes on every damned thing that goes wrong in your life?"

Romero felt the burn coming through the phone. He could kick himself. "Okay, okay. I get it. I'm sorry. It's been a long week. Monday at eleven. My office or yours?"

"Mine. I can't drag confidential files all over the place. Chief Suazo doesn't want anyone at State Police headquarters knowing the case is being considered for review."

"What do you mean?" Romero thought he'd better feign interest.

"Well, supposedly there was a cover-up and the Department is still trying to live it down. Credibility plays a big part. All they need right now is to have it splashed all over the media and put everybody involved on alert."

"All right, I'll see you then." He held on to the phone a little longer.

○≪

Jemimah flipped her cell phone closed. "Still an asshole," she muttered. The black and white Border collie reclining on the couch perked up its ears.

Chapter Two

Jemimah Hodge lived at Peach Springs Ranch, a five-acre spread a few miles north of Cerrillos, New Mexico, at the base of the Ortiz Mountains. The rustic '70's era ranch house had been remodeled to fit her needs. Although favoring Dallas because of her thriving psychology practice, she'd longed for a place where life didn't move at such a rapid pace. The Santa Fe area had been her first choice. Less than a month after settling in, she scored a job with the County.

Jemimah's duties as a forensic profiler for the Sheriff's Office had changed considerably over the past year. She was now the Chief Forensic Psychologist, a position created with her in mind and accompanied by a substantial raise in pay. She reported to both the County Sheriff and the State Police Chief. She respected them both, but Sheriff Medrano was responsible for bringing her into law enforcement and she held him in the highest esteem.

On Monday Jemimah awoke early. She hadn't seen Detective Romero for six months and, based on their recent conversation, it was obvious his feelings for her hadn't changed. She still sensed an underlying tension between them and wasn't sure how she felt. On the surface she wished he hadn't been so open about his desire to start a relationship. Just thinking about it stirred turmoil within her. She was content to keep him at arm's length but knew she couldn't do that much longer. Besides, he was attached at the hip to

Sheriff Medrano. Whether she liked it or not, they were going to be thrown together regularly.

Jemimah exhaled deeply as she stepped into the shower, where she planned to luxuriate for as long as it took to mellow out. Nothing was going to spoil this beautiful day. She toweled herself off and stood inside the walk-in closet. She would have preferred to throw on some jeans and a t-shirt, but pulled out a pair of dark slacks and a long-sleeved white blouse instead—the standard uniform for Department employees. Her five-foot-seven-inch frame was proportionately muscular, indicative of the many facets of ranch life. Her straight blond hair cascaded just beneath her shoulders. Her blue eyes sparkled when she laughed and turned cold as steel when interrogating a suspect.

Driving north on Highway 14, she cranked up the volume on the radio. Steely Dan belted out "Home Again." She sang along, tapping her fingers on the steering wheel. In less than thirty minutes, she arrived at her office in the Sheriff's complex across from the State corrections facility.

A few minutes after eleven, Jemimah stuck her head out the office door, waiting for Detective Romero to show up. She spotted him in the hallway next to the Sheriff's office engrossed in conversation with a flashy brunette. The woman flirted and edged closer, as if she was going to do him right there under the water cooler. Disgusted, Jemimah returned to her desk, rearranged the note pad and stapler, fumbled through her daybook and wound her watch. As she reached for the phone to reconfirm the time, she knocked the coffee cup over and felt a stinging sensation on her leg. Hot liquid continued to roll off the table before she could grab a paper towel to wipe it up. She was bent over, cleaning up the mess, when the knock on the doorjamb startled her.

"Hey, Jem. How's tricks?" Romero was smiling broadly. She realized he'd been checking out the view of her derriere.

"Fine," she said. Her voice was flat. It didn't escape her

that he was in a good mood, his testosterone level probably elevated from dallying with the woman in the hallway.

"Am I interrupting something?" he asked.

"Not anymore," she said abruptly.

"What's that supposed to mean? I thought we had a meeting scheduled, and here I am, right on time."

Jemimah remained silent. *Oh crap. How am I going to dig myself out of this one?* Last thing she wanted was for him to think she was capable of feeling a smidgen of jealousy.

"I'm sorry, Rick. I spilled my coffee. Can we start over?" She tossed the soaked paper towels into the trash, wiped her hands on a new one and reached out to shake his hand as he leaned forward to embrace her.

"Sure, if you insist." He threw his arms up in mock indignation. He sat across from her and stared for a long minute while she gathered her papers into a stack. She wished she'd bothered to put on some makeup; however, the way he was looking at her, he was definitely not finding fault with her appearance.

She nodded and smiled, touched her fingertips to her hair and said only, "I insist." She could see that simple statement surging through him, creating a false hope that things might eventually turn out all right after all. Not in forty moons.

Their meeting went from bad to worse, until Jemimah fabricated a headache. It was going to be an uphill battle for them to rekindle their working relationship.

He couldn't stop looking at her and she couldn't look him in the eyes.

"I'm sorry, Rick. I guess I don't have my ducks in a row on this one. Let me get in touch with you when I have more time to review the file," she lied.

"Sure, sweetness, whatever you say," he said on his way to the door.

"I'm not your *sweetness*," she muttered under her breath,

slamming the desk drawer shut. Jemimah covered her eyes with her hands. "What's wrong with me? I can't stop thinking about him and yet the minute he comes near me, I turn into Attila the Hun. Whether I like it or not, I'm going to have to sit down with Dr. Cade and figure this one out."

&

Romero sat in his cruiser before taking off. He was thinking about Sandra Gorman, the woman in the hallway, an FBI agent assigned to work with the department. He had limited experience with the FBI, although Sheriff Medrano had related a few horror stories. Medrano trusted no one outside his department except Chief Suazo.

His last run-in with the FBI involved the kidnapping of a District Judge. Medrano had a history with the kidnapper and had been working toward negotiating the release of the victim when the FBI pulled the case out from under him. The head agent cited jurisdictional differences when the media leaked the news that the kidnapper was holed up two miles from the Santa Fe County border. This transferred the jurisdiction to the State Police, who immediately called in the FBI, much to Medrano's chagrin. Medrano's efforts to stall the agent in charge from storming the area while he negotiated with the kidnapper were fruitless, and the judge and the kidnapper were both killed in crossfire.

Earlier that day, he'd cautioned Romero about watching his step when dealing with FBI agents. *Even the pretty ones.*

Chapter Three

It was difficult to compare Sandra Gorman to other female Detectives. Brilliant and self-assured, she hadn't become an FBI Special Agent by standing on the sidelines. She had enviable instincts and a cunning nature, which allowed her to wheedle out vital information during interrogation. The regional office had assigned her to work with Romero on a case involving a local pharmacist murdered while attempting to protect a rape victim. In addition to Romero, she would be meeting with other department heads to develop and implement communication procedures between the FBI and local authorities. She was thirty years old with a Kewpie doll face—doe eyes and pouty lips she played up with cherry red lipstick. Mesmerized by her eyes and lips, most people didn't notice her weak chin, partly because of the perfectly bobbed hair designed to frame her face just so. And of course the body, displayed to maximum effect with clothes that skimmed every exaggerated curve.

Always aware of the impact of her stunning looks, she found that a short intro to Detective Romero in the hallway at the County offices served to whet her appetite. She sensed the need to know more about this handsome specimen of local origin.

A few days later, on the pretext of reviewing her case notes, she stopped by Romero's office. His vehicle wasn't in the parking lot, and she wasn't inclined to wait for him to show up. She had plans to sit by the pool at a Santa Fe hotel where she was staying while the local FBI office arranged for permanent housing during her month's stay. Maybe she'd hit the bar first. Who knew what delicacy she might find hanging around there.

Romero's assistant, Clarissa, sat at a desk eating a glazed chocolate doughnut as she gave Sandra the once-over. Casually dressed as Sandra was, even a secretary with a mediocre wardrobe could see that her clothing had designer labels. Obviously, she was used to a lot of attention.

Sandra handed Clarissa her card. "I'm here to see Detective Romero, is he available?" she said.

"Sorry, he's at a meeting. I don't expect him to return to the office for at least a couple of hours," said Clarissa, pretending to have a heavy workload as she rearranged the files on her desk.

"Thought I'd take a chance anyway and familiarize myself with the area. We're going to be spending a lot of time together on this case, you know. Never realized we'd be working way out here in the boondocks, though. Isn't there at least a Starbucks close by where one can get a decent cup of java? There's one on every corner in San Francisco."

Clarissa gazed at her through hooded eyes. FBI or not, she could see this woman was a spoiled California girl. "Nearest coffee house is about fifteen miles north of here, next to the mall in Santa Fe. If you're going to hang out around these parts, you can either bring your own or drink the sludge we brew up every morning."

"Yuck. I'll remember that, *Clarissa,* is it? Now tell me about Lieutenant Romero. Is he married or anything? Can't imagine a hunk like him being out on the open market." Sandra pulled a chair close to Clarissa's desk and sat down. She smoothed her hair with a well-manicured hand.

Clarissa's phone rang. Before she took the call, she

scribbled a date and time on a piece of paper and handed it to Sandra. Waving her off, she said, "Sorry, I have to take this call."

Sandra shot her a look, snapped the paper out of her hand and headed for the door.

"You've got the wrong number." Clarissa spoke into the phone while she looked Sandra straight in the eye. As she hung up, she wore a smile of satisfaction.

She was fiercely loyal to her boss. When she heard that Detective Romero had been promoted to Lieutenant and was being assigned to take over the reins of the newly commissioned satellite office, she jumped at the chance to become his assistant. She had spent the last ten years working at the main Sheriff's Complex.

The job in Cerrillos was perfect for her. Not only did she prefer the solitude of the area, she didn't mind the daily drive.

Clarissa was a homebody and preferred to keep company with her two cats rather than be thrust back into the dating scene. She had done enough of that in the '80s, dancing until dawn at the Sheraton Lounge, which featured popular rock bands. A rocky marriage had further dampened her spirits. Someone who looked like Sandra Gorman didn't do much for a woman's self-esteem.

Chapter Four

As Romero drove into the gravel parking lot in front of the station, his arms were loaded with case files, bathroom supplies and coffee. He motioned for Clarissa to open the door.

She took one of the bags and set it on the desk. Known for her inability to keep things to herself, Romero's long-time assistant accosted him as soon as he walked toward the storeroom. "That curly haired FBI woman was here to see you. Gave her an appointment for Wednesday. She's got the sweets for you, Boss." She winked at Romero as she reached out and took another grocery bag from his arms.

"Dear Clarissa, always so tactful, straight for the jugular. Watching Dr. Phil hasn't helped you much. Let's put these supplies away," he grunted.

"Got her sights aimed right at you, sweetheart. I could hear that biological clock of hers from a mile away: tick-tock, tick-tock." She stood next to him, waiting for a response.

"I was introduced to her a few days ago at Sheriff Medrano's office. She's FBI, Clarissa. Not going to be interested in a home-boy. We're going to be working on a few cases together, that's all. Satisfied?" Romero waved her off. "Don't you have filing that requires your attention?"

Clarissa persisted. "Considering the size of her salary, you could probably retire to a big house in DC or Frisco. Play golf with your buddies all day," she knocked an imaginary ball onto an imaginary green, "while she's out fighting crime."

He shook his head. "You've been watching too many CSI reruns, Clarissa. She's no more interested in me than I am in her. Strictly business."

"Make sure it stays that way. My vote is with the Mormon lady." Clarissa shook her finger at him. "She's more your style."

"Don't go holding your breath on that one, either," Romero said. Although ostensibly bantering, he was dead serious.

"Trust me, boss. There's chemistry there. I know about these things. Roaring fire ready to be stoked." She poured him a cup of coffee, taking longer than usual to stir in the sugar.

"Are we done here, Clarissa? Get back to work," he said.

She gave him a mock salute and returned to her desk. She stared at the computer screen for a moment and then Googled Sandra Gorman's name, hoping to find some juicy tidbit. No use. FBI kept their people tightly reined in, she figured. Clarissa knew Sandra's type. That kind of woman could charm the rattle off a snake. Sandra Gorman wasn't going to get near her boss—not if she could help it.

Chapter Five

Detective Romero trudged out of his office into the bright morning sunlight, slid his sunglasses on and made his way to the cruiser. He was headed to Santa Fe for a meeting with the County Commissioners to plead his case for an additional deputy.

Romero glanced up to see a uniformed State Policeman leaning on the driver's side fender. Captain Jeff Whitney. *What the hell did that arrogant son of a bitch want?*

Whitney's syrup-soaked greeting annoyed Romero. The way he stood, he seemed to be waiting for a camera to snap. An avowed womanizer, Whitney took great stock in his appearance. He was tall and slim, but muscular and tanned in all the right places. A sometime spokesman for the State Police, he was always ready for a photo op. As was generally the case, ultra-dark glasses kept his eyes and his expression shielded.

Romero took a long drag of his cigarette. He smoked Marlboros, although he cringed when the Marlboro-smoking cowboy appeared on television commercials. The guy was no more a cowboy than some of those wusses who hung around the old tavern in Madrid. He fumbled for his keys, irritated that Whitney was still standing there, blocking his path.

CR

Whitney spoke first. It didn't escape him that Romero appeared none too happy to see him. Never had, not since

Whitney began putting the moves on Jemimah from the first time he set eyes on her last year. He was pretty sure she was attracted to him, too. Didn't matter a bit to Whitney. He was all about the chase. As long as it wore a skirt, he would chase it. If the skirt put out, even better. It exasperated him that he had never been able to get her in the sack, but Romero didn't need to know that. Whitney extracted a pack of cigarettes from his shirt pocket, casually ripped out the tinfoil lining, took out the last one and crumpled the package. He was tempted to toss it on the ground. He knew that some poor slob of a DWI offender ordered to civic duty would pick it up tomorrow on his rounds. It chafed his ass that that the publicity oriented female magistrate judge constantly castrated offenders by making them wear pink satin baseball caps while gathering litter along the highways. Nonetheless, one of these days he'd like to testify in court with her wearing nothing but a pink hat.

"Lieutenant Romero, thought I might catch you here," he drawled. His eyes squinted in the bright sun as he removed his sunglasses, replacing them almost immediately.

"It's where I work, Whitney. What do you want?" Romero relit his cigarette, pausing while he took another long drag.

"Just need a few words with you," Whitney said. "Won't take but a few minutes of your time."

"Come back tomorrow. Office hours are over." Romero proceeded toward his vehicle.

Whitney stepped in front of him. "This is off the record, Romero. I don't want an appointment."

Romero pressed the key lock and opened the driver's side door of his cruiser. "I'm already late, Whitney. You've got two minutes."

"Scuttlebutt has it that the Sheriff's Department is working on a cold case from a few years back. Heard anything about it?" Whitney said.

"Nope. Not a word. Nothing's come across my desk. What's it about?" Romero's face expressed no interest.

"State Police officer's wife killed in an auto accident on the way to the hospital. Pretty cut and dried. Case was closed years ago. Don't know why the Sheriff's Department would be getting involved at this late date."

"Got me. That all you wanted, Whitney—information?"

"Pretty much."

"Why don't you ask your own department, if this is one of their old cases?"

"Did. Nobody knows a thing."

"Well, there's your answer. Probably nothing to it," Romero said.

"Maybe. Maybe not."

"Sorry I couldn't be of much help," Romero smiled as he glanced at his watch.

"Sure you are. Thanks anyway." Whitney turned and walked toward his cruiser, flicking his cigarette butt into the bushes lining the driveway.

Had he imagined the spark of recognition in Romero's eyes? Whitney wondered if the lieutenant knew more about the case than he was letting on. No matter. He'd catch him somewhere and beat the information out of him if he had to. A greaser like him had no business being in law enforcement.

CR

Romero stepped into his vehicle. He knew exactly what information Whitney was digging around for. Jemimah would have to watch her step on this one.

Chapter Six

Jemimah had met Detective Romero quite by accident. In the springtime last year, she had been riding her horse near the San Lazaro Indian ruins. She heard a shot echo out into the canyon. That led her to an injured Tim McCabe, and her frantic 9-1-1 call brought Romero to the area neck to neck with the ambulance. The event catapulted her into an unfolding murder case and an eventual job as a forensic psychologist with the Santa Fe County Sheriff's Department.

It was Jemimah's lucky day when she spotted an ad in the local newspaper. The job was right up her alley. Her office in Dallas regularly handled cases involving criminals in need of psychological treatment rather than incarceration. Little did she know the position would also force to face her own emotional issues.

A year ago, Jemimah could easily have fallen in love with Detective Romero. What red-blooded woman could resist? He was on the most-wanted list of every single female in the Department. But first she needed to resolve her own issues related to her staunch upbringing in a Mormon community. She had escaped, but the scarring on her psyche remained buried deep inside. Another hundred visits with Dr. Cade, her long-time therapist, and she could entertain ideas of entering into a relationship, although by then Romero might have moved on. Maybe she would eventually gather up the courage to talk to him about it. Oh sure.

By the way, Rick, I've been screwed up most of my life.

You know, living among a bunch of old men married to teenagers, and terrified that I would be the next one chosen—with my family's blessing—for sacrifice on that altar.

Could Romero still be attracted to her after all this time? She had resisted his every effort to get closer. He knew very little about her except what little he had gleaned from their being thrown together at work.

She took another sip of her drink. Maybe she would talk to him. Maybe. But probably not.

It was at times like these when she recalled her childhood—the queasiness she felt in the pit of her stomach as she overhead the men in the meeting room next door to the Hodge family home in Utah discussing the young women being primed for marriage. She imagined them casting lots to see which one they got. It creeped her out no end. Many of the girls were younger than she. Her saving grace was a chronic skin condition that caused her face and neck to erupt in red blotches. She saw now that it had been a turnoff. Good thing, too. She would rather die than obey the rules her father promulgated in the strict Fundamentalist sect that he headed.

Her mother would now be in her mid-fifties. No telling how many young wives her father had added to the group since she'd left. She kept that curiosity in a boarded up compartment of her head. She had traveled full circle since the day her mother and one of the other wives drove her to a Las Vegas skin specialist for an experimental treatment. That skin condition was the only reason she had still remained unmarried at the ripe old age of seventeen.

She'd slipped away as her mother arranged for payment at the desk. She shuddered to think what would have happened if she hadn't found a small window of opportunity to pull it off. *Would she ever be that courageous again?*

It was getting late and Jemimah hadn't eaten supper. She reached over to pet Molly, the sweet Border Collie she'd rescued from the animal shelter when she bought her ranch. Jemimah filled the metal bowl with tap water and went to the refrigerator. She pulled out a loaf of bread and jars of almond butter and raspberry jam to prepare a sandwich. She nuked a turkey dog for Molly, who patiently watched as it cooled on the counter. Her dog food bowl was overflowing with kibble, but Molly preferred people food and knew her owner was more than happy to oblige. Jemimah sat cross-legged on the couch and downed the last of her drink. She flipped through the TV channels one more time. There was little to hold her attention, and she drifted off to sleep on the couch.

Jemimah awoke with a start. The television set was still on, a loud commercial message garbling on the screen. She had been dreaming about walking across the San Lazaro Indian Ruins in the field next to Medicine Rock. Huge boulders were rolling down the mountain toward her from every direction. She could hear drumming in the background as someone pulled her to safety.

Momentarily disoriented, Jemimah groped her way into the bedroom and flopped onto the bed, hoping to avoid revisiting the recurring dream.

Morning seemed hours away.

Chapter Seven

After serving eighteen long months of a two year sentence, Carlos Romero waited in the release room just beyond the main entrance to the Adult Corrections Center. The facility was on Highway 14, the Turquoise Trail, a few miles from the interstate. He was dressed in an ill-fitting brown polyester suit, white shirt and black loafers. The manila envelope he clutched in his hand contained his watch, driver's license, and thirty-two dollars.

Carlos had been incarcerated on a trumped-up drug charge, presumably intended as payback. His brother, Sheriff's Deputy Detective Rick Romero, had dared to break up a drug cartel just outside of Santa Fe.

Although he considered himself more or less innocent, Carlos had admittedly stopped at the dealer's house to pick up a small bag of weed. The informant knew Carlos was coming by but didn't bother to inform Detective Romero. He wasn't about to get himself killed for making it too easy on the cops. Besides, he planned to make a few extra sales and then haul ass through the kitchen before the shit hit the fan. He didn't much like being arrested, but sometimes it was the only way to retain his cover and earn his play money from the cops. The charges against the informant were dismissed for lack of evidence and Carlos went to jail for possession of marijuana.

Detective Rick Romero drove into the lot of the corrections facility in his personal car, knowing that if he used his official vehicle, his arrival would be on the five o'clock news. One never knew when Channel Thirteen's watchdog reporter might be skulking around looking for something to hang the Sheriff with. He preferred to keep things simple.

It had been a while since Romero had been inside the prison. Following his promotion to Lieutenant, he relegated the duty of prisoner delivery to his deputies. The civilian area of the prison consisted of rectangular compounds within concrete slabs. Vaulted doors controlled by high-tech devices concealed behind bullet-proof glass clanged as they slid open and closed. The outside yard was the size of two football fields, and was encircled by high walls and razor wire fences. Inmates milled about, ever vigilant of their surroundings. Armed guards walked side by side along the perimeter. The whole area reeked of a musky mix of testosterone and urine. A disembodied voice in the background barked orders over the loudspeaker. Fluorescent lights cast a harsh blue pall over the entire setting.

Rick Romero had mixed emotions about picking up Carlos today. He was fully aware of the grudge his brother held against him for letting him go to prison. Romero had stopped his weekly visits over a year ago because of Carlos's constant bitching over the events leading to his arrest.

Their last conversation had been a heated one. "Damn you, Rick, you could have told me you were going to do a bust that night at Chunky's house." Carlos's voice seethed with animosity.

Romero gave as good as he got. "Well, what the hell were you doing buying pot from a known dealer? You could have picked up a bag anywhere on the street."

"Hey, man, it was just a spur of the moment thing. Me and Gina were going to grab some Mexican take-out and then go to her house and watch DVDs. You should have been covering my back," Carlos said sullenly.

"Look Carlos, my hands were tied. Once the bust went down I didn't know who the hell was in there. We ran all the plates in the driveway and, since you were driving her car, there was no way I could have known." Romero had been over this time and time again with his brother. He couldn't understand why it didn't soak in.

"Yeah, right. If I was one of your white-boy Gringo friends, I would have gotten off with just a ten dollar fine and a smack on the wrist," Carlos retorted.

"If you hadn't already had a few misdemeanors on your record, you might have. Don't throw the blame on me, Carlos. With your rap sheet, the judge could have given you a harsher sentence and let you rot for five to ten." Romero was no longer smiling.

"Oh, that's right, Rick." Carlos looked like he was about to explode. "Go ahead and say it. You spread that bullshit about 'don't do the crime if you can't spend the time.' Well, I'm doing the time, because you're too chicken-shit to help me get out of here."

"What the hell is it you expect me to do, Carlos? I got you an attorney who explored every possible avenue. The judge didn't buy it." Romero was completely flustered. Their conversation was going nowhere.

"What I want you to do is to leave me alone. Don't bother coming back here." He motioned for the guard.

Romero stood up to leave. "Okay, brother. If that's the way you want it."

"It is," he said, flipping him off over his shoulder.

Romero winced as he realized that conversation of a year ago was still fresh in his mind. He unbuckled his holster and placed his weapon in the trunk. The sunlight seemed brighter than usual as he stepped out of his car. Walking up to the main gate, he flashed his credentials and was directed to an office down a long corridor where he signed in. The guard led him to the holding room, where Carlos sat on a long bench, eyes downcast.

Sergeant Rodriguez walked over to Carlos and tapped his shoulder. "Hey, you, Romero, time to leave. No more free room and board. Get your butt out of here."

Carlos returned a weak smile and reached out to shake his hand. "Rodriguez, I'm going to miss your smiling face. Call me. We'll do lunch."

"Yeah, yeah. Go on. The Lieutenant is waiting for you." He patted him on the back and escorted him into the hallway.

Romero hesitated for a moment before reaching out to grab his brother's arm and giving him a quick embrace. He hoped Carlos' attitude had lightened up now that his sentence was complete. They walked out to the car in silence. The sound of the steel gates closing reverberated in his ears.

"You hungry? We can stop and get something to eat if you like," Romero asked as he buckled up.

"Nah, I just want to get out of these clothes and into a hot bath. I've had about a million showers and I'd like to soak my butt in water up to my neck for a change," Carlos said.

Romero saw him eyeing the metallic green exit signs for the new bypass and a dozen or so cracker box office buildings and chain stores that had shot up in the past year. The world changed awfully quickly. Romero kept his eyes straight ahead, occasionally glancing in his brother's direction. It wasn't in Carlos' nature to be so quiet. Jail time seemed to have mellowed him, at least temporarily.

"If you want, you can stay at the house for a while. You can sleep on the couch in the spare room until you decide what you're going to do," Romero offered.

"All right. Okay by me. I'm not sure how I'm going to feel without the lights shutting down at nine o'clock." Romero saw that his brother's smile was forced. He imagined that Carlos wasn't sure about anything at this moment. He was just glad to be out, wanted to get as far away as possible from the prison.

"You're going to be all right, Carlos. Just give it a little time," Romero assured him.

"Whatever you say, brother. Whatever you say."

Carlos's fellow inmates had been incarcerated for lesser crimes than those in the more secure areas of the facility. He kept the knowledge to himself that his brother was a detective; otherwise he would have been an easy target for violence. It had been a grueling test of his resolve, spending each day trying to avoid a confrontation that could land him in lock-up and lengthen his sentence. On his early release for good behavior, he figured Rick probably wasn't too happy about having to take him in.

"You don't have to worry about me, Rick. I'll find someplace to stay," he said.

"Yeah, right, Carlos. How much do you have in your pocket? Twenty bucks? Won't buy you a decent meal, let alone a place to stay. I already said it was okay for you to stay at the house for a while. Don't make it a big deal."

"Okay, but just until I get back on my feet." Carlos remembered that when they'd been teenagers, Rick had always had to bail him out of something or other. "In about a month the prison will send me a check for the work days I earned on the prison work program."

"What's that amount to, about sixty cents an hour?"

"Believe it or not, I logged quite a few hours working in the metal shop."

"Tell me you weren't making license plates," Romero snorted.

"Actually I worked on a big contract, assembling circuit board transformers. Learned quite a bit about electronics."

Carlos was surprised that Rick was actually interested in hearing what he had accomplished.

"And don't forget you can't be hanging around anyone who might lead to trouble. Women included. There's a whole list of no-nos on your release papers, so get familiar with them," Rick said, bursting his bubble.

"There we go. Isn't it a little soon to be reminding me that I just got out of prison? We're just, what, maybe ten miles from the gate? How many times am I going to have to repay my debt to society, Rick?" he said, his fist banging against the door.

"Give me a break, Carlos. I did everything I could possibly do for you."

"Except keep me out of prison."

"I'm a cop, not a magician." Carlos knew the effort Rick was expending to keep his voice calm.

"What happened to all my stuff? Anything left?" Carlos sensed he'd better change the subject. No use in alienating the only person admittedly on his side.

"Not much. I went over and cleaned your place out after the trial. I salvaged as much as I could. Mostly clothes. Sold your car to pay the attorney. That's pretty much it. Everything's stored in the garage."

"I'm not sure how long I want to hang around Santa Fe. Not much of a future here." Carlos rolled the window down, feeling a sudden wave of anxiety.

"No, not unless you get a job. And no matter what, you still have to see a probation officer on your own, Carlos. I'm not going to babysit you. Enough said."

Carlos remained silent for the remainder of the drive. He was fully aware of all the rules. At the moment all he wanted was put the prison experience behind him. He didn't ever want to relive the nightmare of being handcuffed and shoved into the back seat of a police car. His early scrapes with the law had involved petty theft and shoplifting cartons of cigarettes from the grocery store. He never imagined he would ever do something to cause him to be arrested and taken to jail. His parents would have been so ashamed.

Yeah, he had learned his lesson, but his dear brother couldn't seem to see that.

Romero pulled out onto the interstate and drove the eleven miles to St. Francis Drive in silence. He had expected a little more conversation but wasn't surprised at how easily interaction with Carlos degraded into a full-blown shouting match. Carlos had never opened up to him, even before they'd thrown him in jail. He turned off the main road onto a side street. Cottonwood trees on both sides formed a green arch over the unpaved road that led to a small adobe house in the South Capitol area of Santa Fe. This was the house they'd grown up in. It now belonged to Rick, and Carlos had never been too happy about that.

Chapter Eight

It took Carlos a week before he awakened without feeling disoriented, expecting a loud booming voice over the PA system to announce breakfast. After driving around Santa Fe, he headed out toward Cerrillos. He felt the freedom of the breeze blowing through the roof of the new Toyota Corolla that Rick had helped him buy with a loan and the money he earned while in prison. He zipped into the handicapped space in front of the Sheriff's Department satellite office. He figured not too many people on crutches or wheelchairs needed to come way out here to see a deputy.

At that same moment, Jemimah Hodge left the building strolling toward her car. She shot Carlos a *tsk tsk* look, which he returned with a big smile.

"My brother's the boss here," he explained coyly, putting out his hand. "I'm Carlos Romero. You work here?"

"No, I'm Jemimah Hodge. Rick—Lieutenant Romero—and I occasionally work together." She returned his smile. He knew the effect of his looks on women.

"Well, then. I'm sure we'll be seeing a lot of each other." He flashed another toothpaste ad grin.

CR

Clarissa did a double-take as Carlos sauntered toward her desk. Last time she'd seen him he had been a scrawny teenager about to graduate from high school. Now, twenty years later, he was the kind of guy her daughter referred to as *eye candy.* Her boss was handsome in a rugged kind of way, but Carlos was definitely gorgeous.

"Clarissa, long time no see. Still keeping all the criminals on the straight and narrow?" He bent down to kiss her on the cheek, lingering there for the effect he knew it would have.

"Hey, Carlos. I heard you were on the loose again. How are things going?" She didn't see any need to skirt the issue of his incarceration, a fact that didn't escape him.

"So far so good. Any chance of me seeing my brother the Loo-ten-ant for a sec?"

"He's kind of busy right now, Carlos, but I can slip him a note. Have a seat. Help yourself to the coffee. It's fresh. Another hour and we paint the floor with it." She pointed him in the direction of the kitchen.

Clarissa tapped on Detective Romero's door. He was sitting at his desk across from FBI Agent Sandra Gorman, discussing recent developments in the case she had been assigned to collaborate on. Clarissa knew Sandra's poor opinion of police work in this area. By Sandra's standards, the case they were discussing was run of the mill and should have been solved months earlier.

"Excuse me, Boss. Your brother would like a moment with you," Clarissa said.

"Agent Gorman, would you mind stepping out into the reception room for about five minutes?" Romero said. "I have a couple of matters to discuss with my brother and then we can finish up here."

Sandra blinked her long eyelashes at him. Clarissa muttered under her breath, *oh brother*, her hostility automatic but subtle.

"Sure, I need to freshen up a bit. I don't know how you can stand this heat." Sandra walked out of the room, flapping the front of her sheer blouse against her chest and fanning her face with an empty file folder.

"You can go in now." Clarissa motioned to Carlos,

whose eyes followed Sandra into the bathroom, causing him to walk into the doorjamb.

∝

"Wow, who's the pretty lady?" Carlos said. "She's almost as pretty as the blonde I met out in the parking lot. Said she's working with you on a case. I must say, brother, you sure get some hot chicks going in and out of here. I assume they're not the criminal element. I'm kind of liking that Jemimah chick. What a bitchin' name. Remember that syrup bottle shaped like a woman that used to sit on Grandma's table?"

"That was *Aunt Jemimah* and I doubt Dr. Hodge would appreciate being likened to a black mammy."

"So can I get her phone number?"

"Don't mess with her, she profiles criminals for a living," Romero said to his brother, an edge to his voice. He meant to say *she's taken*, but knew he couldn't back up that statement.

"Hey, Man, I'm clean, I'm straight, paid my dues on those trumped up charges. Besides, she's got some nice junk in her trunk. *Oooh, Mama!*" Carlos burst into laughter.

Romero forced a laugh. "She's way out of your league, Carlos. You'd never make it to first base."

"Have you made it?" Carlos flashed another toothy smile. "Is that what this is about? You've got the hots for the chick and can't take a little sibling rivalry?"

"Never mind, Carlos. What do you want? I've got a lot of work to do." He was annoyed at himself for feeling threatened by his brother. *Chrissake*, he'd only been out for a couple of weeks. It was natural for him to hit on every woman he met. He had a lot of catching up to do to revitalize his playboy persona and he wasn't wasting any time. Already the bathroom vanity at home was filled to capacity with the latest men's hair products and colognes. Smelled like a damned beauty parlor.

"I was thinking maybe if you could loan me the money I

can find myself an apartment, seeing as how you're holed up at Mom's house," Carlos said.

"Hey, it's *my* house now, Carlos. Mom left it to me—you were already well on your way to becoming Loser Boy. You can stay as long as you want, just don't get too comfortable. The place isn't big enough. Once you find a job and get on your feet, it's adios time." Romero chucked his Styrofoam coffee cup into the trash.

"That's what I'm talking about. Loan me some cash so I can start looking around. Shouldn't take too long to find me a bachelor pad on the east side."

"I helped you get your new wheels, isn't that enough? And have you even bothered to check out the prices on the east side? You weren't in jail that long, Carlos. Anyway, I don't have any extra cash to give you. Just paid my taxes. Sell that piece of land that Mom left you."

"I was hoping to hold onto it for a while and sell it to a rich developer who can build a couple of million dollar houses on it. But yeah, you're probably right," Carlos said.

Romero tossed him a business card. "This guy's a realtor. Give him a call, tell him you're my brother. We're done here, Carlos. I need to get back to work. We can talk about this later."

"Yeah, sure, later," Carlos said.

∞

Carlos walked back into the reception room. As if on cue Sandra jumped to her feet. Clarissa had made a point of introducing them. Perhaps she'd observed the sparks flying between them earlier, or maybe she just wanted to divert Sandra's radar from Detective Romero.

There was nothing discreet about the way Sandra threw herself at Carlos. It was her way of proving a point. She knew it would probably take too much work to get the detective interested in her since his mind seemed to be otherwise occupied. Besides, this brother looked ripe for the plucking. If she couldn't have the man she wanted, she'd have the man who wanted her. Simple as that.

ભ

It took Carlos a week before he summoned the courage to dial her number. She answered on the second ring.

"Sandra Gorman here." Her voice had a sexy lilt to it.

"Carlos Romero here," he mimicked.

She laughed. "What a nice surprise. I wasn't sure you'd call."

"Hey, how could I resist? I feel like the new kid on the block. I was thinking of sending you flowers, but figured that might not be a good idea," he said in his meekest voice.

"I love flowers, anytime, anywhere," she cooed.

"Well, maybe next time." He could almost taste the honey dripping from her voice.

"I'm glad to hear there will be a next time," Carlos said.

Perfect, he thought. A chick who likes flowers for no reason at all.

"Am I interrupting anything? You sound like you're driving through a tunnel."

"No, no, just getting out of the shower."

"Whoa, Nellie. Do you want me to call you later?" he said.

"No, I'll just put you on speakerphone while I dry off," she chuckled.

The visuals were challenging, but Carlos managed to assuage the lump in his throat with a sip of water.

"Are you still there?" she gushed.

"Yeah, something just went down the wrong pipe."

Chapter Nine

Off duty, Detective Rick Romero looked forward to the quiet contemplation he experienced sitting at home in front of his mother's small shrine and the plaster of Paris statue of the Christ child in the center. The Santo Niño de Atocha was a popular religious figure in New Mexico. Romero kept a votive candle burning at the foot of the shrine on the small table. It was one of the few Spanish-Catholic traditions he observed. His mother frequently prayed to this revered saint who she charged with keeping her two sons out of trouble.

Santo Niño, Santo Niño. A mis hijos, da carino. Cuida los de dia; cuida los de noche. Holy child, Holy child, lavish your loving attention on my sons. Watch over them by day and by night.

Throughout most of his childhood Romero had listened to his mother recite this little prayer. She never doubted that whatever she prayed for would come to pass. Because it had always been her practice to kneel in prayer each day, her husband joked that she had a direct line to heaven. No need for her to worry about their daughter, Maria, a jewel from the day she was born, unlike her rambunctious brothers.

It was in this part of the house that Romero could converse with his parents, both deceased for more than twenty years. It was a sacred silence compared to loud noises that filled the streets of downtown Santa Fe in recent years— honking horns and low-riders cruising the plaza, hydraulics pumping to the rhythm of music blaring from the bandstand in the park. His parents married in the 1950s. From the moment they met, they had been inseparable.

Unfortunately, John Romero's social drinking spiraled out of control fifteen years into the marriage. It wasn't a surprise to Mary's family when her husband eventually died of alcohol related liver disease, leaving her with three children to raise. Fortunately Romero was level-headed and helped his mother considerably. Some years later, his still broken-hearted mother suffered a diabetic stroke and never recovered. It would have taken too much effort. She just wanted to die and join the husband she missed so terribly. There was little the children could do to make her happy. She died on Christmas Eve that year. Her older sister came to live with them until they were grown and on their own. Another sister took the young Maria to be raised with her daughter.

Romero had painstakingly restored the small three bedroom adobe house his grandparents had built in the 1930s and given to his parents on their wedding day. The kiva fireplace was flanked by two old handcrafted tin sconces made by one of his great-uncles. The long *vigas* on the ceiling, hand-hewn by a relative, had a patina that presented as the color of amber honey. The original hardwood floors had been waxed and polished to a deep luster, covering years of footsteps that had pattered across them. The walls were plastered an off-white and hand-polished to a high sheen.

An old hand-carved Spanish Colonial *Cristo* hung on the wall in the living room. Romero's partner, Tim McCabe, told him it was worth a small fortune to a collector. A number of years ago, Romero had been curious about its value and drove to Taos to meet with a well-known dealer. The man offered three hundred dollars for the piece, explaining that it was made by a lesser saintmaker and therefore worth very little. In fact, the dealer was willing to pay that much just to take it off his hands.

"Good thing you didn't listen to him," said McCabe. "You can buy a new Mercedes convertible with what that carving is worth in the present art market."

Romero wasn't about to part with this family heirloom—not that a new car wouldn't be nice to have. The 1995 Subaru his co-workers called a yuppie wagon was starting to wane in performance.

The small backyard of the house overflowed with wildflowers. Hollyhocks leaned gently against the plastered adobe wall, a cultural contrast to the bright purple wisteria sneaking over the west wall from the neighbor's yard. An oak tree provided abundant shade over the patio. The whole scene was authentic Santa Fe style. Overall, it was a pleasant setting, unpretentious and homey and Romero loved every inch of it. Nothing, including his brother, could spoil the way he felt.

Although it was inevitable that Carlos would stay with him for a while until he could settle down in his own place, it couldn't be soon enough for Romero. His brother had a knack for playing the guilt card every time he wanted something. As the older of the two, Rick had been expected to take care of his little brother. Keeping Carlos interested in school and off the streets proved to be a daunting task. He still felt the need to take care of Carlos, even though they were both in their late thirties. Right now Carlos hadn't been around for a few days and that was just fine with him. As long as he wasn't back in jail.

Romero figured he was probably still hanging around Agent Gorman like a pit bull in heat.

Chapter Ten

Sandra Gorman took a long sip of coffee and inhaled deeply, slowly massaging the back of her neck. She was nervous about seeing Carlos again. Damn it, at times like this she wished she hadn't quit smoking. She could sure use a cigarette about now. She also wished her cup of tepid coffee was a martini.

Sandra carried herself with an air that suggested she had been born to money. Her path to law enforcement had been a short but convoluted one, accomplished primarily by her extensive education. It didn't hurt that her father knew people in high places.

Other than a stint in the nation's capital, this was her first assignment away from FBI headquarters in San Francisco. Her task was simple, such as it was. She was to develop a system that would focus on providing a smooth flow of intelligence data from the FBI to local law enforcement and vice versa. In the past, local departments hadn't bothered to inform the FBI of their findings until after their own investigation was complete. She was assigned to set up guidelines to ensure agents were called into the initial stages of a case. She was well aware that an inherent distrust of the FBI existed in all law enforcement agencies in New Mexico. She felt the tension as soon as she displayed her badge. If she'd been in charge, she would have picked a better assignment for herself than this hick town.

At this moment, she didn't really care what her superiors

thought about her. They governed her movement from nine to five. After hours, she was on her own. Besides, it would probably take a month for idle gossip to trickle down to the brass, and by then she'd be headed off to another assignment. She turned her full attention to the task of the moment, commandeering a waiter to order a martini.

Sandra hated sitting alone, waiting. Not just here, anywhere. The hotel and restaurant were on the outskirts of town, on a hill overlooking the bright night lights of the Santa Fe airport. She tried to convince herself she had randomly chosen this particular place for them to meet. It was out of the way, catering mostly to travelers waiting to catch the next flight out. She had to admit, if only to herself, that she knew it was unlikely they would run into anyone she knew.

The restaurant served the best seafood in the area and she was allergic to shellfish. Already she could imagine the tell-tale itch in her throat just from looking across the room at the apprehensive lobster floating in the murky water of the fish tank.

The busgirl loaded plates into the plastic bins and casually wiped the tables. A roll of pink flesh oozed over the tight waistband of her jeans. She was wearing a tank top too short to cover a smaller woman's navel, let alone one so abundant. Sandra wondered why a high-end restaurant would permit such an obvious fashion faux pas to be on their staff. She had to be related to someone in command. That was the only explanation Sandra could come up with as she tried to distract herself from yet another fantasy about sex with Carlos.

An elderly couple took their time ambling toward the unoccupied table near the window.

Carlos walked in behind them. Not a hair out of place. No five o'clock shadow. Not even a single wrinkle in his Kelly green shirt, which brought out the color of his eyes. Sandra was accustomed to seeing him in jeans and a t-shirt. His pale prison complexion was gone; he was nicely tanned, his dark black hair smoothed into place by a touch of gel. A big smile formed on her face. She felt like a coyote in a henhouse, knowing she was his first date in eighteen months. The many hours spent engaged in long phone conversations had quickly propelled them toward this dinner date. During their first conversation, Carlos told her he had been in jail for almost two years on a fabricated drug charge intended as a message to his brother. The sincerity in his voice made a believer out of her.

The thought that her superiors wouldn't look kindly on an agent dating a felon, trumped-up charges or not, kept gnawing at her, but then she'd tell herself she didn't give a damn. Besides, she was horny and missing her on-again-off-again boyfriend in San Francisco. And as each day passed, it appeared more and more likely he wasn't willing to deal with the long separations dictated by her career, a career she wasn't about to give up in favor of domesticity. She wasn't that kind of girl.

Over the past two weeks, she'd learned Carlos was a complex creature, with a voice that on one hand could instantly soothe and on the other hand command attention. His astrological sign was Gemini, the twins, and Sandra suspected both Dr. Jekyll and Mr. Hyde resided under his skin. What a contrast to his brother, the detective, who was so distracted she hadn't been able to garner any interest from him at all.

Carlos waved as she looked up. He slid into the chair next to her, bent forward slightly and kissed her on the neck, interrupting her self-flagellation.

"Mmmm, you smell nice," he whispered. "Hope you haven't been waiting long. There was a jam on the bypass. Truck lying on its side." He traced a line across her lip with his finger.

Sandra felt a blush radiating from her neck to her cheeks.

It was a good thing the restaurant was dimly lit.

He moved his chair closer to hers. The waitress handed them menus and placed two glasses of water, two goblets of wine, and a basket of miniature loaves of bread on the table. For just a millisecond, the symbolism from her long forgotten Catholic upbringing unnerved her.

"This is a great place. Last time I was in this area it was just a tract of vacant land adjacent to the airport." His voice was ecstatic, "Great location for a restaurant, overlooking the ninth green."

"Are you into golf?"

"I'd like to be, but I prefer a more strenuous sport." He put his hand over hers. "You know this is my first official date in over two years," he said slowly. "I hope I don't embarrass you with my enthusiasm. I feel like a teenager."

"Not to worry," she laughed. "I'm pretty relationship-challenged myself."

"No steady beau?" he asked, eyebrows raised.

"Not really," she lied.

"C'mon, a pretty lady like you surely must have lots of opportunities." His knees rubbed against hers.

"Well, most of the time I'm either on a jet, at a crime scene, or in a meeting or a classroom. I'm lucky to have time to change clothes between jobs."

Carlos laughed. "You think that cramps your style ... try wearing a prison jumpsuit, or just having one in your past. You'd be amazed how quickly that scenario discourages serious dating."

She slowly blinked her eyes, flashing rows of long lashes. "I'm so glad we have this opportunity to get a little better acquainted."

"So am I." He squeezed her hand. "Talking on the phone has been nice, but face-to-face is nicer."

The warm flush reappeared on her cheeks. "That's so true." She wanted to say *Body to body would be even nicer.*

The waitress aimed the hot plates between them and set the food down. She seemed to have a burr up her ass. Maybe someone had stiffed her for the tip. Sandra put on her most condescending smile. "Thank you; we'll call you if we need you."

The main course was sitting across from her and he looked delicious. She had all she needed right there.

Chapter Eleven

Romero struggled to regain consciousness. It took a few minutes to realize he wasn't home in bed. The moistness of the ground beneath him saturated his shirt. A bright moon shone overhead, peeking through the tall pines. He moaned. The pain in his head pulsated as he tried unsuccessfully to pull himself into a sitting position.

He tried to remember where he was and how he got there. A wave of nausea hit as he braced himself on the ground, smelling the pungent aroma of juniper and piñon around him. As he channeled his inner Rambo and pulled himself to his feet, a gush of blood streamed down his shirt. *Jesus*, he'd been shot.

The moonlight lit the way toward the outline of a vehicle in the distance. As he drew nearer, he realized it was his cruiser. He fumbled through his pockets for the keys and finally found them on the seat. Gripping the steering wheel to pull himself up into the vehicle, he pushed the key into the ignition, grateful that the engine kicked over. Pain shot through him as he backed into the brush and jerked as the tires drove over felled branches on the road. He remembered walking on the forest service road to Los Cabreros Mesa about ten miles from the Cerrillos substation, about to approach a dark sedan with an obscured license plate, when a bullet tore through his shoulder, knocking him to the ground. Whoever had shot him must have figured he was dead. They hadn't even bothered to take his revolver or his wallet. They'd probably been hiding drugs or contraband, but he never had a chance to find out.

Detective Romero drove the vehicle onto the interstate in the direction of the hospital in Santa Fe. He felt around for his cell phone and speed-dialed Detective Artie Chacon to meet him there. The drive felt considerably longer than the twenty minutes it should have taken. If he pulled over to the side of the road he would pass out. Finally, he spotted the lights of St. Vincent's on the hill up ahead. Blood continued to ooze down the front of his shirt. Detective Chacon's cruiser lights flashed at the front entrance to the hospital.

The emergency room at the hospital was jammed. The lobby was filled to capacity, the ailments ranging from swine flu to some kid who swallowed the head of a plastic action figure. A man wearing a camouflage jacket held a bag of ice on his swollen arm, while another stared ahead and conversed with nobody in particular about the bats hanging from the ceiling. The woman next to him looked at herself in a hand mirror. Romero figured she was inspecting the most recent batch of cuts and bruises inflicted by her live-in boyfriend. Detective Chacon ambled up to the ER nurse.

"Excuse me, Nurse," he said.

"Sir, please take a seat," she said stiffly. "The emergency room is on a first come-first served basis, and unless your emergency is more urgent than everyone else's, you'll just have to wait. We're seeing as many patients as we can at the moment."

Undaunted, Chacon flashed his badge, reached over and pulled Romero's bloody shirt open to expose a gaping wound. "Sorry, Ma'am. This won't wait."

The nurse hollered for the orderly to bring a wheelchair, plunked Romero down and directed them to a curtained-off cubicle in the far corner. She took Romero's vital signs and proceeded to cut away his shirt. Over the intercom, they heard the ER doctor being summoned.

Romero felt the room spin. He closed his eyes.

Three hours later he was spread-eagled on a bed in the recovery room, still woozy from the anesthesia. His head throbbed, but he was determined to get up. He pushed the blankets away, swung his legs over the side of the bed and attempted to stand upright, almost toppling the I.V. stand. The orderly caught him before he crumpled to the floor.

At ten o'clock the next morning, Romero awoke feeling out of sync. Nurse Jenny Kimball was checking his blood pressure and poking a thermometer into his mouth. He could clearly see that all he was wearing was a blue pin-striped hospital gown. His eyes widened as he saw a syringe coming toward him.

"Now hold still, Detective Romero. We need to draw some blood to make sure you haven't developed an infection," she said.

"Ouch," he said with a grimace. "So where are my clothes?"

"I asked your friend to bring some clean clothes and underwear. He said he'd be here by the time you were released," she said.

"Hope that's soon." He couldn't tell which was pounding harder, his head or his shoulder. He put his hand over the patch where the bullet had been removed. "Feels more like I've been hit by a truck than a bullet. Probably shot with a damned hunting rifle."

"You're lucky that shoulder's still intact," Nurse Kimball said. "We've worked on some pretty messy hunting injuries, and sometimes the patients leave here without a lot less skin and bone than they came in with."

The aide wheeled in a tray of food and placed it on the portable table. The smell of eggs nauseated him. "Eat," the nurse admonished. "We don't like our patients leaving here hungry. Bad for our reputation."

"Not hungry. I need to get out of here," Romero said.

"Not until the doctor releases you. So you might just as well relax," she said as she lifted the cover on the plate, exposing a Denny's style breakfast.

He took a bite of the syrup smothered pancakes and almost hurled. "I can't, sorry. Stomach's upset," he said.

"Probably the Hydrocodone. It affects some people that way. I'll note it on your chart," she said, sliding the tray out of reach. "It could also be the anesthesia. Sometimes it takes a few days to wear off."

Romero looked up as Dr. Amos Hillyer came into the room. "Detective Romero, I can't say it's good to see you again," he said.

"Have we met before, Doc?" Romero asked, still foggy. The inside of his head continued to thump with every movement.

"I operated on Tim McCabe last year when he was shot out at San Lazaro Pueblo. You were investigating the case," he said, pulling back the bandage for a look at Romero's shoulder.

"Ouch. Oh yeah, I remember now. You sewed him up," Romero groaned.

"How is old McCabe doing? I heard Sheriff Medrano corralled him into working with the Department on a few cold cases. Bet his wife pitched a fit on that one." There was a touch of sympathy in his voice. "She was just getting used to him being retired."

Romero winced as the doctor yanked the tape around the wound to remove the gauze dressing. "Good man to have on board. We don't often have the opportunity to work with a seasoned police officer like him."

As he made a few notations on the chart, Dr. Hillyer said, "The good news is, Detective Romero, that the injury wasn't as bad as it initially appeared, otherwise you'd be looking at an extended stay. Bullet chipped the acromion and lodged on the edge of the muscle above the clavicle. Quite a bleeder, and you're lucky to have gotten here when you did."

"Can I have that in English, Doc?"

"Zinged the collarbone," Dr. Hillyer said with a grin.

"Assuming this isn't fatal, the bad news is ...?" Romero anticipated the worst, looking at his chest for another wound.

"The bad news is that you're going to have to ease off your workload in order for this to heal properly," he said flatly. "Even though we've managed to sew you up quite nicely, if you don't take it easy there's a good chance you'll end up losing the flexibility in your arm. If that happens, the Sheriff is likely to assign you to desk duty for six months, and I know that wouldn't bode well with you."

"Okay, Doc. I can do that, I promise." Romero felt as though he was seven years old.

"Of course I could have Nurse Ratched here fax a copy of these instructions to the Sheriff," he said, winking at Nurse Kimball.

"No, no, Doctor Hillyer. Honest Injun. I'll do it," he said.

"All right, Detective, I have your word. And oh, here's a present for you." He tossed a small plastic bag on the bed. "Thought you might want this as a souvenir."

Romero was surprised at the contents of the bag. The Doctor obviously knew how long it would take to get the bullet back to forensics if the proper channels were followed. He planned to take it to the lab first thing. The guys should be able to provide a make and model of the weapon in short order. And then he would get some rest. He reached over and shook Dr. Hillyer's hand.

"Thanks, Doc."

"Hopefully I won't be seeing you in here again unless it's on official business, Detective."

"I'll do my darndest, Sir."

Romero heard the familiar ring of his cell phone somewhere in the room. The nurse reached into the drawer and handed it to him. "Hospital policy is no cell phones, but since you're a police officer, I think they'll make an exception."

Jemimah's name flashed on the caller ID.

"What happened to you last night? You were going to call me about the Ilfeld case," she said, obvious irritation in her voice.

"Sorry, ouch." Pain shot through him as he switched the phone to his other ear.

"Are you all right? Where are you?" she said.

"I'm sorry, Jemimah. I ran into a bit of trouble last night, never made it back to town. Couldn't call you, either, was on my back for a couple of hours."

"You don't have to describe your sexual exploits, if that's what you're talking about," her voice stiffened.

Romero tried to laugh, but the pain intensified. Artie Chacon walked into the room and tossed a bag of clothes onto the chair. "I'll explain it to you when I see you. Right now I need to get out of this hospital. I'll call you later."

Before Jemimah could mouth the word hospital, the phone went dead. Her feet ached from jumping to conclusions.

Two hours later, Romero's head still felt like it was going to explode. The codeine had finally worn off. He popped some extra-strength Tylenol into his mouth and wolfed down a beef burrito. Another cup of hot coffee and he was good as new. A hot shower would do him a world of good, but that would have to wait until the stitches were removed. He settled for a quick shave. His knees were still shaky. He wobbled into the living room as the phone rang. It was Detective Chacon.

"You all settled in, Rick? Doing that take-it-easy thing the doctor ordered?" Romero knew Artie was grinning from ear to ear.

"Yes, Mother. Doing exactly that. Did you get any hits on the vehicle driven by the asshole who left me for dead?"

"Nope. Whoever did it hightailed it out of here. All we

got is tire tracks. 'Course they're still looking. Sorry, *Comandante.*

"How about the slug; any info on that?" Romero asked.

"Nah, the tech said there weren't enough identifying marks on it to make a determination of the type of weapon."

"That sucks. Some asshole's floating around out there scot-free waiting to take another pot shot at me."

"Could just be something random. Who the hell knows?"

"Yeah, that's a huge consolation," Romero snipped. "I'll be sure to include that in my report."

"*Eeholay*, Boss. Take it down a notch. Maybe you need to be getting some of that rest the doctor prescribed. Take a chill pill."

"Save that pachuco slang for another occasion, Artie."

"I can see you're not in the mood for company. Catch you later, alligator. I have a domestic complaint to serve back in Waldo."

Romero was contrite. No use taking his frustrations out on his right-hand man. "Make sure you put your full body armor on."

"Will do, Boss."

Romero was no stranger to being caught in the crossfire of angry husbands, wives and boyfriends. He too sported a few scars from random bullets. Truth be told, he'd rather eat dirt than approach a domestic situation, especially in the Cerrillos area.

Chapter Twelve

Jemimah was attractive, tanned and fit. Her blond hair sparkled with golden sun streaks. Her skin was smooth, her nose had a slight upturn, and her lips were movie-star perfect. In spite of this, she found it difficult to socialize out of her comfort zone.

She'd spent her childhood in a vacuum. As an adult she longed for an imagined intimacy that had never been a part of her parents' relationship. In her early twenties she'd had a short-lived misalliance with a fellow student at UCLA. Realizing she had married a man just as domineering and controlling as her father—a man who, like her father, considered her unworthy of attention—she broke it off.

In the ensuing years Jemimah buried herself in her studies, becoming a straighter than A student, sorority leader and valedictorian. On a warm afternoon in May, she walked across the stage to receive her diploma and the accompanying accolades. Some years later she earned a PhD. On each of those occasions, there were no proud parents in the audience, smiling siblings or great aunts. She had left them all behind after her escape at age seventeen. Every one of them had played a part in her imprisonment, and she preferred not to look back.

Because of her discarded past and the wary way she lived, Jemimah had few complications to prevent her from pursuing her ambition to become the best in her field. That year she relocated to Dallas, hung up her shingle in a small office complex and set about building a practice counseling patients in need of her psychological services.

Within five years, Jemimah built up an enviable following. A Children's Court judge, impressed by her handling of cases, began to refer juvenile offenders to her office for psychological profiling as a deterrent to future criminal activity. Court administrators also took note of her success rates and soon juvenile and adult referrals for evaluation began to outnumber her private patients. Jemimah embraced the philosophy that soft-core criminals could return to society within a reasonable period of time after a series of intense psychotherapy sessions. She had the ability to elicit more information in five minutes than most people could in an hour.

Each year as her criminal caseload increased, she found herself spending more hours assessing criminal behavior and presenting her findings in high profile court cases. Although her practice was both lucrative and successful, by the time she made the decision to move to New Mexico, she was also overworked and overwhelmed. It wasn't long after she became a criminal profiler in Santa Fe that things started to get personal.

As Jemimah pored over the Ilfeld case file, nothing screamed out at her. She wasn't any closer to unraveling the mystery than she had been when she first flipped through the file. In retrospect, she was certain that over a year ago, Captain Jeff Whitney had approached her with what she perceived as genuine enthusiasm about working with her on this same case.

"I could use your help on this, Jemimah," he said. "The Ilfelds were friends of mine; he's a fellow officer. There's a lot of scuttlebutt about an argument, something went wrong, they got in a wreck on the way to the hospital. I know for a fact there's nothing suspicious about her death. It was an accident. But for some damned reason, the Chief's under a lot of pressure from her family to reopen the case. I know there's nothing to it, but I still have to go through the motions."

A few months later Jemimah was in a hotel room in Denver after a long day of gathering evidence when the phone rang. It was Whitney.

"Jemimah? Glad I reached you," he said.

"What's going on, Whitney? I'll be back in Santa Fe tomorrow, can't this wait?" She thought he was calling to ask her out again. She wasn't in the mood to play telephone footsies with him.

"This will just take a minute." Abandoning his usual flirtatious tone, he kept his voice cold and somber. Even the exaggerated southern drawl was noticeably missing.

"All right," Jemimah said. "I have to catch a flight at the crack of dawn, so make it short."

"I've been reviewing that case I asked you to take a look at, and I've decided there's nothing there to pursue. I took the liberty of picking up the file from your office," he said.

"Well, that could have waited until tomorrow," she said. "And by the way, Whitney, I don't appreciate your picking anything up from my office without my being there. There were a few things about the case I wanted to review with you, and I was planning to do so in the next few days."

"Did you not hear what I just said, Jemimah? The case is officially closed, period." And then he hung up.

Case closed. End of story. Jemimah had never heard from him after that. He'd never even stopped by her office to spend a flirtatious fifteen minutes trying to get her to go out on a date. No more candy or flowers. She was stumped. She was beginning to think Whitney's friendship with his fellow officer might be the key to the case, but she couldn't figure out how. He was a veteran police officer who had been on the force for over twenty years. Granted, she did suspect he was on the ruthless side and lived by his own set of ethics—that's probably why she was initially drawn to his bad-boy image— but from a professional standpoint, she doubted he was capable of serious crime. He had too much at stake.

Now that the case had been reassigned to her, she knew the answers were somewhere in that file. She studied each page, putting everything in chronological order. At the end of the timeline, she was back at square one. As she jotted down Rose Ilfeld's date of death, it suddenly dawned on her that the statute of limitations for filing criminal or civil charges was coming up in less than ninety days.

What did Chief Suazo suspect that Jerry Purcell, the previous Chief of Police, hadn't? Or was he somehow indirectly involved? Suazo had intimated to her that a blue wall had been thrown around the investigation. Almost every piece of evidence, incriminating or otherwise, had mysteriously disappeared from the file. There was virtually nothing to base a new investigation on. But on the bright side, unknown to anyone but Chief Suazo, a microfilmed duplicate of the case file resurfaced in former Chief Purcell's unclaimed storage files.

The evidence in the case, sparse as it appeared, had been relegated to four plastic bags. Blurred handwriting on a yellow Post-It note caught Jemimah's eye. It was a notation of a call made to the DA's Office by one of the EMTs at the scene, whose name had been crossed out. She made a note to get someone to decipher the name and check on his whereabouts. Jemimah also found it odd that nobody had ever retrieved any of Rose's personal effects. Her husband would have been the only person authorized to do so and she wondered why he hadn't.

One small plastic bag contained Rose's wedding ring. Another held a gold chain with a small diamond cross. Surely these items would have had at least sentimental value to a grieving husband.

Chapter Thirteen

Jemimah waved down the pretty girl in the hallway lugging the burrito basket. Fishing out a *Carne Adovada* special and a soda, she returned to her desk. As she wolfed down the tortilla clad spicy mixture of grilled pork and red chili, she continued her review of the evidence—or lack of it—in the Ilfeld case.

She swallowed hard as she thumbed through the autopsy photos. It unnerved her to think she might be allowing her emotions to get the best of her. Why this victim? What was it about her that tugged at Jemimah's heart strings? Rose Ilfeld would have been about her own age today. A random thought wove through her head. Rose Ilfeld had an uncanny resemblance to her birth mother, Clara Wells.

Clara had married her childhood sweetheart, Jason Hodge, in Utah in 1970. Jemimah was born two years later. Jason Hodge was a fifth generation Mormon and had recently moved the family to Hildale to join a fundamentalist sect. Before long he began to embrace the concept of polygamy. By the time Jemimah was twelve, her father had three wives and six more children. There was no doubt in her mind that her mother would have preferred to be the only wife, but she stood in silence, agreeing with her husband every time he proposed the addition of a new young wife into their midst. Jemimah struggled to get along with the new women who were sharing her father as though he was a prized rooster.

At fifteen, Jemimah was astounded to learn that her

second mother Kathryn was only a few years older than she was. The same was true of the third addition to their family, a beautiful dark-haired young woman named Rebecca, who later confided her fears that she might not be chosen as the new wife. Within six months, she was expecting a child, which would bring the count to eight. Eight siblings who were strangers to Jemimah, as she preferred to distance herself from them.

" 'Not be chosen,' are you demented?" Jemimah said. "I would die if I was forced to get married so young!" But all young Mormon girls were not headstrong and independent like Jemimah. The vast majority followed the precepts of the church and its leaders to the letter. Each was fully aware of her position and what was expected. Jemimah couldn't wrap her brain around the concept of multiple wives.

"Oh, no, Jemimah. I am so fortunate I was chosen. I will be a good wife and mother," Rebecca said.

"A mother?" Jemimah was aghast. "You're hardly older than I am. I surely wouldn't want to be a mother. Not now, maybe never!"

Her father stormed into the room and pulled her aside. "You will keep your disrespectful remarks to yourself, Jemimah. Your fate is sealed as long as you are a member of this family, and you should be grateful a good man will eventually provide for you, despite the unappealing condition of your skin."

Jemimah snapped herself back into the present. She reached up and touched her cheek. The skin condition her father had referred to over twenty years ago had miraculously cleared up within months of her escape from the community.

Refocusing her attention on the case, she scoured the file for a phone number and called Rose Ilfeld's mother to schedule an appointment for the following day.

Early the next afternoon, Jemimah parked her car on the street in front of a multi-storied north side Santa Fe home. She rang the doorbell and in moments was greeted by Pamela Davis, who smiled graciously as she led her into the living room. The room was tastefully furnished in leather, chrome and glass. The walls were painted in apricot hues, and the carpet was a deep cobalt blue. The Andrew Wyeth painting over the fireplace was easily worth a million dollars. It seemed out of place among the cheaply framed prints that surrounded it. The entire scene was a cross between ostentatious and an attempt to reflect a perceived social status.

Pamela was neatly dressed in a flowered print blouse and dark pants. Her auburn hair was coiffed in an updo that was outdated but fit her self-contained personality. The chunky turquoise and silver jewelry she wore appeared cumbersome on her small frame.

Jemimah gazed at the row of photographs on the mantle. The plush carpet cradled her sandaled feet. A large plasma TV flashed images of recent presidential interviews.

"The one on the right is my daughter, Rose," Pamela said as she brought in the coffee service.

"She was very beautiful," Jemimah offered.

"Rose would be thirty-eight next month." She poured two cups of coffee and motioned for Jemimah to sit at the small table on the deck overlooking Hyde Park, a juniper dotted area of Santa Fe just below the Ski Basin. "I can't believe it's coming up on ten years." Her voice cracked as she reached for the cup. She cleared her throat.

"Mrs. Davis, Pamela, can you tell me what Rose's daily schedule was like?" Jemimah said.

"Yes, of course. Rose was a homebody. Ever since she was a little girl playing with a bevy of dolls, she talked about being married. She loved to cook and work in the garden. Even in the wintertime she spent most of her day cultivating plants in the greenhouse. She belonged to the Garden Club. She read a lot. She kept up to date with world affairs."

"Was she a very social person?"

"Oh, yes. She enjoyed being around people and she loved to laugh. My daughter had a marvelous sense of humor. She wasn't a party girl, per se, but she was outgoing and liked to have a good time. Don didn't care for that kind of thing. He was mostly into sports and preferred to hang out with his buddies on the police force."

"Did they socialize much as a couple?"

"Rarely. Only if it was a work-related event, anything to do with law enforcement—retirement dinners, awards ceremonies and the like. I assume he probably took her out on her birthday or anniversary. She never said much about it." Pamela continued to stir her coffee. The spoon whined against the inside of the china cup.

Jemimah could see how difficult it was for her to discuss her daughter. She also sensed an underlying resentment toward the couple's son-in-law. "Your daughter was still fairly young when she died. How long did she date Don Ilfeld before they married?"

"As I recall it was a fairly brief courtship, if you can even call it that. At that time Rose was in the process of completing her master's thesis at the university in Albuquerque when fate threw them together. By then Don Ilfeld was a seasoned police officer and was conducting a criminology seminar at the college. Her roommate introduced them. She brought him home to meet us that Thanksgiving. I had a few misgivings then," she said. "Not only did my husband and I feel he was too old for our daughter, but I thought he was extremely narcissistic. Everything he said was about himself. One of her friends told us he considered himself quite a ladies' man and usually played the field, going out several times a week, hanging around singles bars. I wish he would have stayed out of our lives and hers."

"Did you express your misgivings to Rose?"

"No. Before we had an opportunity to really get to know him better, they flew to Las Vegas and got married. On the surface, my daughter appeared to be happy, but I knew her better than anyone. She wasn't about to admit she had made a mistake, especially since she knew both my husband and I disapproved of him."

"So she never expressed any doubts or dissatisfaction with her married life?"

"No, but once they settled in, her social life slowly came to a standstill. She spent more and more time at home. That's what he preferred." Pamela reached for a box of tissues. "I'm sorry, this is so emotional for me," she said, "having to relive everything once more is still very painful. I'm not sure I'll ever get over it."

Jemimah placed her hand on Pamela's wrist. "I understand, and I'm sorry, but I have to ask this. Do you have any idea why Don Ilfeld or anyone else would want your daughter dead?"

Pamela cringed every time his name was mentioned. "There were a couple of things we thought about. After the funeral, we heard rumors that Don had accumulated a few gambling debts and was afraid Rose would find out," she said.

"Why so?"

"Well, on his salary and with the purchase of the new house, they were barely scraping by. He was having trouble paying off his bookies and they were applying pressure on him, State Policeman or not."

"Did Rose have a job?"

"Oh, no. She wanted to work, and she was qualified to hold down a well-paying position with a number of local organizations, but Don made two things very clear. He didn't want children and he didn't want his wife to work. He was too macho for that. We found out about an insurance policy he bought a year before she died. The policy paid double indemnity for accidental death, and coincidentally that's how the coroner ruled it, an accident," her voice trailed off.

"Speaking of the coroner, what had you heard about him?" Jemimah said.

"Not much, other than what was reported in the newspapers. Our attorney said he had a heart attack and died about a year after Rose's death, so if we had filed a wrongful death lawsuit against Don, we would have had nothing to back it up except the written record. As I understand it, the coroner's report is very cut and dried."

"Didn't a national television network take an interest in the case? The file doesn't say much about it," Jemimah said. "I must have heard that somewhere."

"Oh yes, I had forgotten that. An investigative reporter for a major network profiled the case. She was scheduled to interview the coroner about his findings. She left the hotel, headed to the Coroner's house, and was picked up by the State Police a few blocks away on a frivolous DUI charge. She spent the night in jail. By the time she bailed out and attempted to reschedule their appointment, the coroner had been found hanging from a tree in the apple orchard on his property. A tad too convenient, if you ask me. More coffee, Dear?"

Jemimah clasped her hands. "No, thank you. I think I've already taken up enough of your time. I'm going to continue looking into that business with the reporter. Maybe I'll find something in another file. Pamela, I do want to caution you about discussing this case with anyone, particularly the news media. My task is to provide the Commission with sufficient information for them to determine whether or not the investigation into your daughter's death should be reopened. The fewer people aware of what's going on, the better. Everything I'm looking into is confidential. We don't want anything, no matter how insignificant, to leak out."

"I understand. You will get back to me if you discover anything pertinent?"

Jemimah assured her she would. Pamela walked her to the door and gave her a fond embrace. Jemimah felt the interview had been fruitful.

Chapter Fourteen

As she walked down the driveway to her car, Jemimah reached into her satchel for the keys. Out of the corner of her eye, she noticed a dark sedan parked across the street, its engine idling. Before the ensuing thought could register, she heard shots ring out and felt herself pulled to the ground.

"Stay down, Jemimah," a voice hollered.

The sedan drove straight at them and veered onto the road as Tim McCabe fired three shots at the vehicle.

"McCabe! Oh, my God, who was that?" Jemimah sat up, craning her neck.

"Don't know, Jem, but I managed to get the last three numbers off the back plate. Someone had tried to blot out the number with dirt. Looked like a Lexus. Not sure if any of my shots hit home. It all happened so damned fast." He helped Jemimah to her feet. "Are you all right there, Honey?"

"Yes, of course. I'm just a little shook up. This doesn't seem like the type of neighborhood for a drive-by," she said. She caught her breath. She knew very little about gang activity, but figured this was exactly what they might do.

"Doubt if it was gang-related, Jem," McCabe said.

"Are you serious?" she brushed herself off as she rose to her feet. She thought briefly of Rick and his brush with death. They had spoken a few times, and he'd reassured her the incident was probably random. The department was still investigating, but had little to go on. Romero didn't believe he was in danger, but she still worried about him. Even though she couldn't seem to go forward with the relationship, she cared very much about his safety.

McCabe walked Jemimah toward her car. "When you first drove up to the Davis house, did you notice anything suspicious in the area?"

"I remember looking around the street, taking in the architectural style of the houses and the pristine front yards. I think I would have noticed someone watching me," she said, "particularly since I was looking for the house number I had written on my tablet. So I traveled down the street looking at every house in the neighborhood. Some of the houses appear to be on double lots, so the numbers didn't run consecutively. In fact, I passed the house the first time and had to double back. I'm pretty sure I would have noticed anyone else in the neighborhood. It's not a very long street."

"You didn't see that dark sedan parked anywhere on the street?"

"No, I don't believe I saw any vehicles, not in the driveways, either. It didn't seem to be the kind of neighborhood where people park their cars on the streets. Not with so many double car garages."

McCabe pressed on. "Well, have you noticed any suspicious looking characters anywhere else you've been lately?"

Her eyes widened. "Are you implying that some weirdo has been following me? I think I would have noticed. I'm not that oblivious to my surroundings."

McCabe could see Jemimah was sufficiently spooked without him adding to it. "Look, Jem. If you don't mind, I'll be checking on you from time to time. Just as a precaution."

"I don't think that's going to be necessary, Tim. This is probably just random, don't you think?" Her eyes were even wider than before.

McCabe tried to hide his uncertainty with a smile. "Could be, but we're not taking any chances. Don't want anything to happen to my favorite girl."

She, too, forced a smile. "All right, but hopefully this will be temporary. I don't feel comfortable having a bodyguard. Nothing personal."

"I'll be so discreet you'll never know I'm around. But I do need you to keep your cell phone on you, not in your purse, not in your car, not in your desk drawer. Keep it in your pocket at all times."

"You're scaring me again, McCabe," she said.

"Sorry, didn't mean to. Law enforcement suggests it's safer for women to carry their phones on their person. Easier access in case of an emergency. Just passing it on, for what it's worth."

"Yes, Sir. Will do my best."

Jemimah glanced toward the Davis house. All the lights were off. No use alarming Pamela any more than necessary. She clearly hadn't heard the shots fired, nor come to think of it, had anyone else, or someone would have called 9-1-1. The neighborhood seemed to have a Stepford Wives appearance, cookie-cutter houses occupied by cookie-cutter families. She waved at McCabe from inside her car.

ଔ

McCabe's shoulder felt a little sore from the tumble he'd taken when he'd grabbed Jemimah. He was looking forward to a good soaking in the hot tub in his back yard. As he headed home, he called Detective Romero to report the event.

Romero was infuriated. "Who the hell is stupid enough to attempt running someone down in broad daylight?"

"I got three numbers off the plate. Don't know if it will do any good. I'll run them through when I get to the office," McCabe said.

"Hey, you've already had a full day, Tim. Go home. We can go over this in the morning," Romero said. He hung up the phone and reached for the prescription bottle in the drawer. The pain in his shoulder wouldn't let up and it was becoming more difficult to stay focused.

Chapter Fifteen

Tim McCabe sat at a desk at the satellite office in Cerrillos. Detective Romero tossed his keys on the adjoining desk.

"You're up pretty early this morning, Tim," Romero said, adjusting the bandage on his injured shoulder.

"Yeah, Rick. Couldn't wait to get in here. The DMV database processed the three numbers from the vehicle that careened toward us yesterday. It yielded over ninety matches, eight of them dark sedans." McCabe shook his head. "It's not a narrow enough search and there's not a Lexus in the bunch. Dead end." He leaned back in his chair and stretched. "No point in going any further. I'll have to come up with something else. I was no damned positive it was a Lexus—but hell, all these new cars seem to look alike. Could have been a Caddy, or even a Buick."

"Stay on it," Romero said. "Bound to be something to connect one of them. You sure it had a New Mexico plate?"

"Happened pretty fast, but yeah, I'd recognize that same old drab yellow plate with red letters anywhere. It's about the most unattractive license plate in the U.S."

"Might be stolen plates, you know. Hard to say," Romero said. "That's a hell of a lot more info than we have on my shooting."

Tim McCabe was an old-fashioned lawman originally from Idaho. He had been retired for years and relocated to Santa Fe about ten years back. He and his wife Laura ran a trendy art gallery on Santa Fe's east side and lived on posh acreage near Museum Hill and Sun Mountain. They were avid collectors and generously supported the art community. He had a strong law enforcement background and kept up to date on new developments in the field.

McCabe had been appointed by Sheriff Bobby Medrano. The two men had known each other for more than twenty-five years when they both worked security for the horse racing track at Ruidoso Downs in southern New Mexico. McCabe married the boss' daughter and returned to Idaho. Medrano moved on to a career in law enforcement. Last year, much to Laura McCabe's dismay, Sheriff Medrano pulled a few strings to get Tim appointed as Special Investigator for the Santa Fe County Sheriff's Department. He'd been chomping at the bit to get back into law enforcement and jumped at the prospect.

Although Tim had promised Laura it would be part-time, of late he'd clocked a lot more hours at the Sheriff's office than at the gallery, and he readily admitted to himself that he was loving it.

McCabe was cowboy handsome, six feet tall with deep set blue eyes and sandy brown hair, graying at the temples. In his early sixties, with a muscular, suntanned physique, he was aging gracefully. In addition to Wind Medicine Gallery on historic Canyon Road, he owned Indian ruins south of Santa Fe at San Lazaro Pueblo near the town of Cerrillos. Before his recent appointment he had spent much of his spare time digging for artifacts on the ruins. To date he had assisted the Sheriff in solving several crimes, including the gruesome discovery of the bodies of five young women buried in a tunnel on the edge of the Indian ruin property. At the moment he was determined to track down the vehicle that attempted to plow into Jemimah.

Romero interrupted his thoughts. "Come on, McCabe, let's go into town for some breakfast. Maybe another cup of strong coffee will clear your head."

"Doubt it could be any stronger than what you people brew here, but sure, let's go. I'll follow you in my car. No use me driving all the way back. I'll just take my work with me."

❧

The coffee shop was housed in a building a block south of Canyon Road in the historic part of Santa Fe. For three-quarters of a century before its eventual conversion, the building had housed the only grocery store on the east side. The coffee shop shared space with an upscale Santa Fe bookstore. Although the staff changed periodically, obnoxious attitude coupled with indifference, rudeness and nonchalance seemed to remain. It still took ten minutes to get through the line, even for someone buying only the *New York Times* or the *Wall Street Journal*. The young waitress efficiently cleared off a table for them, and by then their order was ready. Romero thought things might be changing for the better.

McCabe's blue eyes peered over tortoise-shell reading glasses. "How's the shoulder, Rick?"

"Guess I can't complain," Romero said, touching it gingerly. "Could have been a lot worse."

"Have you spoken to Jemimah recently?"

"We talked a few times after my accident. I tried her a number of other times after that, but I think she's screening her calls." Romero looked up as McCabe continued to gaze in his direction. He ate a mouthful of eggs and washed it down with a swallow of juice. He wasn't sure how to respond, so he stalled for time by eating. "What?" he finally said.

"Nothing, really. I just hoped you two had ironed out your differences by now."

"No differences to iron out, McCabe. It's pretty obvious her preference seems to be a *don't look at me, don't talk to me, don't touch me* kind of strictly business relationship. I think she has to force herself to be civil to me when we're working together on a case. I can't figure her out, McCabe, and quite frankly—" Romero made a motion over the top of his head. "I'm up to here trying."

"To quote something I heard a long time ago," McCabe said, "the lady doth protest too much."

Romero laughed. "What does that mean, McCabe? You're talking to a beaner here."

McCabe smiled. "It means that when a woman can't make up her mind about her feelings, she raises Cain about everything else. You're damned if you do and damned if you don't. At least that's this old cowboy's take on it."

"You sure about that? I'm under the distinct impression she can't stand to be around me, period." Romero motioned the waitress for a refill. This wasn't exactly the type of conversation he liked to engage in at breakfast time, but he knew Tim McCabe generally spoke his mind and from the sound of it, he wasn't finished.

"Listen, Rick. I've watched you and Jemimah circling each other for over a year now. I saw the sparks fly between you two from the first time she dropped into our lives, and you haven't even gotten to first base."

"Yeah, I remember. But I've tried everything I could to bring her around. Just about the time I imagine we're going to get something going, she balks like a skittish coyote and runs off in the opposite direction."

"I'm not one to break a confidence, Son, but I'm going to give you a piece of advice. Now hold that thought. I need another cup of coffee and a cigarette." Romero knew that McCabe had recently picked up smoking again and had yet to admit it to his wife, although she had commented about the smell of smoke on his clothing.

"I think I'll join you," Romero said. They stopped at the counter to pay the tab and ordered two coffees to go. He handed one to McCabe and headed out in the direction of the open air patio. The sky was clear and the day cool. They sat at a small plastic table near the adobe wall. McCabe leaned forward, elbows touching his knees.

"All right, Rick. Listen up. You know my wife and I consider Jemimah to be like our own daughter. There's something about her that makes you want to hug her and take care of her."

"I hear you." Romero blew a puff of smoke up in the air. An elderly woman sitting nearby with her dogs shot him a dirty look and fanned the area around her face with an imaginary fan.

"Yes, but there's more to it than that."

Romero wasn't sure where the conversation was going, but he respected McCabe and his opinions about life. "Go on, I'm listening."

"Jemimah and Laura have engaged in a number of conversations in our sitting room. A lot has been said that I'm sure she wouldn't want repeated. A couple of times I was relaxing in my favorite spot out on the portal, sipping a glass of Scotch and reading a book, and the two of them had their heads together like they'd been friends for years. Anyway, Rick, without going into detail, what I feel compelled to tell you is that Jemimah had a very difficult childhood growing up in a Fundamentalist Mormon community. I'll let you fill in the blanks, but I'm hoping someday you two will sit down and she'll open up to you about it."

"Something bad happen to her?"

"I'm not saying she was molested or anything. I'm just reading between the lines. You and I have both dealt with enough pedophiles and perverts in our careers to know the damage they can inflict on a child with their mere presence." McCabe took a long sip from his cup. "Had it not been for extenuating circumstances and Jemimah's extraordinary strong will, she would have probably been married off to some old geezer by the time she was fifteen."

Romero was pensive. He shifted his weight in the chair.

"Tim, do you really think there's a chance? I was getting ready to move on and just accept the fact that the most we'll ever be is professional associates."

McCabe snuffed out his cigarette. "Here's the advice I promised. I think you should approach Jemimah a little at a time. Kind of like breaking in a filly. Let her come to you. Keep your reactions to a minimum. Don't spook her. Give her a lot of room, but reel her in a little if she goes too far afield."

Romero chuckled. "That's quite an analogy there, Tim."

"Listen, I'm just an old cowboy with a limited knowledge about women other than my wife, and I'm not even sure I'm an expert on her anymore. But I do know horses, and I know Jemimah knows horses."

"You saying women are a lot like horses?"

"I'm saying Jemimah is intelligent, strong-willed and stubborn. The last filly I broke had those same characteristics. Get the connection?"

"Yes, sir. I think I do."

"Well then, once you can learn to keep from letting her irritate you about every little thing, you might get something going. Now if I don't finish up for today, I'm going to have to appease my own thoroughbred woman who's expecting me home by lunch time. I still need to try to run those numbers through DMV again."

McCabe reached into his pocket for his car keys and took off.

Romero stayed to finish the last few swallows of his coffee and light up another cigarette. Even if Jemimah never did confide in him, his whole perception of her had changed.

Chapter Sixteen

Jemimah felt emotionally drained as she sat on the leather recliner in Dr. Jerry Cade's office in the second story of a Guadalupe Street loft. She fidgeted with her bracelet and stared out the open window into the busy parking lot. Still unnerved by the events of a few days before, she was going on her second sleepless night. Her stomach was tangled in knots. The five or six cups of black coffee she'd downed since that morning didn't help matters. The same thoughts kept circulating through her mind. Who would want to harm her and why? Were they just trying to scare her? Well, they had sure accomplished that. She was scared and didn't know where to turn. Jemimah wasn't a quitter, but she sure felt like throwing in the towel on this one.

Over the years Dr. Cade's office had become a comfort zone for her as he poked and probed into significant events of her life. She knew the layout of the room—where every piece of furniture belonged, where every painting hung—and noticed every speck of dust the cleaning woman missed on her weekly foray through the complex.

Dr. Cade was one of a few practicing Native American psychologists in New Mexico. She'd heard him lecture at a conference about the effects of culture on a patient's psyche and decided he would be someone she could relate to. A cowboy at heart, he usually dressed in a western shirt, boots and neatly pressed jeans with a straight crease running down the front. He didn't wear a gold ring on his finger and he never mentioned a wife. Jemimah admitted to herself she could easily be attracted to him, as he was exactly the type of man she could visualize in her life. Dr. Cade was tall, trim but muscular, and loved horses and the outdoors. The silver streaks running through his dark hair caught the sunlight coming through the window. This was precisely the type of man she would describe if she was filling out a romantic survey in *Cosmo* Magazine—"Find Your Soulmate!"—or an online dating service.

She sighed. *What am I thinking? It would be unethical.* Psychologists didn't date their patients, even if that patient happened to be another psychologist. No exceptions to the rule. While she was in fantasy mode, it also occurred to her that Lieutenant Detective Rick Romero also fit her criteria to a T.

On this occasion she sat in the psychologist's office not thinking of anything or anyone else but herself. As they sat in silence, he waited patiently for her to speak. She had disclosed very few details of her present dilemma to Dr. Cade, preferring to continue to mull it over in her head.

"Earth to Jemimah," he said gently.

"I'm sorry, Dr. Cade. I seem to be more distracted than usual lately." She didn't feel much like being there but knew there was no way she could leave once she sat in the chair across from him. Besides, in her own private practice, it would piss her off big time if a client walked out on her in mid-session for no apparent reason other than they just didn't feel like talking.

Dr. Cade seemed to sense the seriousness of her predicament. "To use a well-worn cliché, Jemimah, you're a bit like a caged animal. You can run but you can't hide. Everything will still be there in the morning, so I suggest we do more than merely minimize the events." He gave her a hard look. "I've never seen you in such a state. You haven't said two words in fifteen minutes, and our session's one-third over. Do you want to talk about it, or are the hummingbirds flittering outside the window more interesting?"

Jemimah clasped her hands. "I apologize again, Dr. Cade," her face flushed. "It's all I can do to stay awake. I haven't slept for the past couple of nights. My head hits the pillow and then I'm wide awake for the rest of the night."

"Just by looking at you, I get the distinct impression you've worked yourself into a state; you're feeling overwhelmed. I can prescribe a light sedative, if you'd like. It would help you get some restful sleep."

"No, no. I'm fine. You know I don't do well on drugs. I'm just trying to make sense of this whole thing."

"All right, then. Tell me what happened, Jemimah. You mentioned someone fired a couple of shots at you."

Her eyes misted as she remembered the incident. "I walked out to my car after an interview. I reached into my bag for my keys. Before I knew it, I was flat on the ground as a car sped by with someone firing shots out the window."

"That must have been frightening."

She continued to wring her hands. "At first I couldn't figure out what was going on; everything happened so fast. And then all of a sudden I was on the grass and Tim McCabe was shielding me with his body."

Dr. Cade suspected she was close to tears but that her sense of professionalism wouldn't allow her to cry. He reached over and took her hands.

"Let's stop here for a few minutes, Jemimah. This whole subject seems to be difficult for you to discuss."

"I'm sorry, even rehashing the details is stressful." She reached for the box of tissues. "I feel embarrassed to be so wimpy."

"Nonsense. Just lean back and close your eyes. Let's try a bit of relaxation therapy."

For the first time in weeks, Jemimah felt herself relaxing to the point of almost falling asleep. Dr. Cade's technique never failed to provide a new perspective. Ten minutes later he directed her to open her eyes. "Better?"

"Much," she said.

"All right, let's move on. You were saying you found yourself on the ground. Is Tim McCabe that old cowboy from Idaho you worked with last year on the multiple murder case?"

"Yes, that's the one. Apparently Detective Romero asked him to keep an eye on me."

"I'd say lucky for you he did."

"Seems that way." Jemimah lowered her eyes. She still wasn't ready to admit or even explore her feelings about Rick. Maybe she never would be.

"Jemimah, try not to block anything out. Tell me what repercussions from this situation are affecting you? I'm referring to deeply embedded emotions, not those on the surface."

She sat motionless, unsure of how to answer. "I think this whole incident has made me feel that I'm not really as good at my job as I thought I was."

"How is that? I thought you were fairly comfortable with your job," he said.

"Oh, not in the technical sense. My credentials are flawless, I'm proud to say, and I know I'm good at my job. What I'm referring to are those deep-rooted feelings you're interested in hearing about." She slipped her left foot out of its shoe and tucked it under her right leg. "Maybe I'm not the kind of person who does well when confronted with the prospect of being shot at by some maniac wielding a gun."

"How do you see yourself at this stage in your life, Jemimah?"

"Well, you know, I generally don't get rattled easily. I know where my strengths lie. But I certainly don't see myself chasing a suspect down the street or slamming him to the ground and slapping the cuffs on him. There are a few female detectives who are trained to do that. But I'm not a detective. Not by any stretch of the imagination."

"So what's changed since you took this job? I remember you were excited about the opportunity to work hand in hand with law enforcement."

"Well, it seems as though within a few weeks after I started with the Sheriff's Department, my job description changed from full-time psychologist to honorary cop. Maybe not on paper, but the nuances are there." Jemimah sighed. "I get the impression I'm always pissing someone off, so they see the need to do me in."

"Go on."

"You remember the prime suspect in the San Lazaro ruins case last year? Followed me home and tried to throw me off a cliff. And here we are again—some lunatic taking potshots at me as he drives by."

Dr. Cade kept nudging her on. "So what does all this say to you?"

"Maybe I need to change jobs?" Jemimah raised her eyebrows, aware that wasn't the answer he was looking for.

"That's a little drastic. Let me make a suggestion." He looked her squarely in the face. "You need to remove your psychologist hat and work with me here. Where else could you put your skills to work, since you know you're good at what you do? Whatever comes into your mind first … don't give it a lot of thought."

She tugged at her sleeves, as though checking to make sure they were aligned on her wrists. "I'd probably end up teaching, maybe transfer into one of the available positions working with new recruits at the Police Academy."

"Would that be enough of a challenge for you? What do you think?"

"I doubt it," Jemimah admitted. "But at least there wouldn't be someone trying to off me. Since I started this job, I've been kidnapped, held hostage, regularly threatened and almost run down by a maniac in a dark sedan."

"For the next few weeks why don't you ask the Sheriff to assign a bodyguard to protect you? Although it sounds like Detective Romero has already done that. Are you certain they were after you?"

"I have information that might blow the lid off a case I'm working on. It involves a couple of high ranking State Police officers. Initially this was all supposed to be highly confidential—oh God, see how easy it is to spread the word? I guess I should just shut-up."

Dr. Cade glanced at his watch. "Jemimah, our time is up, but I want you to promise you'll get some help. How do they refer to it in your circles, backup?"

She grimaced at the cop show reference but smiled and promised him she would.

CR

Dr. Cade wasn't so sure. Jemimah had a stubborn streak that stretched for a mile and he knew that, more often than not, it clouded her vision.

Chapter Seventeen

Jerry Frazier sat on the well-worn beige leather recliner in the living room of his Alameda Street casita. Every cell in his body was riddled with Cancer. His once impressive physique had dwindled down to a hundred and thirty pounds. Although only in his early sixties, he was a mere shell of a man, his skin furrowed and his once abundant hair now thinner than corn silk. The intense suffering he endured had dulled the mischievous glint in his hazel eyes.

A profound desire for redemption gnawed at him. Years of battling his illness had managed to knit him a new conscience. Perhaps this final act of compassion would provide a small window of opportunity to get him into Heaven, an ace in the hole. He had nothing to lose. Lord knows he deserved Hell, but Hell was what he'd been living in for almost ten years, keeping the secret.

The persistent breeze from the swamp cooler raised goose bumps on his forearms. Chemo made his hands and feet feel icy cold no matter what the temperature, compelling him to wear gloves. His life was slowly going down the tubes, the disease sucking up every cent he had. At each opportunity, when he thought he could get away with it, he shoplifted his necessities from Wal-Mart and stole cigarettes from the Giant gas station down the block. Despite the futility of resisting death—there was no doubt in his mind that he would be dead soon—he persisted, willing himself to get up each morning.

Frazier had been married only once. He had grown up in Denver in the 1960s, in an era of free love, pot and acid. He'd subsisted on that for a number of years. Then he met Adriana, who had altered every idea he'd ever had about love. She had been a tall, Spanish-American goddess with jade green eyes and straight coal black hair that cascaded past her waist. Thin but still voluptuous. He'd never desired anyone else. They'd explored LSD, mescaline and peyote. There had been nothing they couldn't do together.

In the spring of 1969, they packed all their worldly goods into his jalopy and headed to Taos. They drove into New Mexico, wound their way across the Rio Grande Gorge Bridge and settled into a hippie commune in the mountains near Tres Orejas. That was his first mistake. His second was believing that there among the Volkswagen buses, the Timothy Leary followers and Joan Baez groupies, he and his first love could build a life. Within a few short months, a younger version of himself strolled into their midst, and in a fog of marijuana smoke, Adriana left his bed and moved to the east side of the communal building they shared with a dozen other couples.

Disillusioned by the turn of events in his no-frills lifestyle, Frazier returned to Colorado and didn't venture back into New Mexico until 1990. He had no more personal contact with Adriana. A while back he heard through the grapevine she was getting ready to sell off her property in a remote village southwest of Santa Fe and move to Washington to join a community headed by a guru she met while attending a conference on legalizing marijuana. Yep, that was Adriana. A little on the flaky side, but great in bed, and always looking for a cause. Frazier figured it hadn't taken much for the group to convince her to move to Washington, lock, stock and barrel. After all, wasn't that what that fellow Applewhite did with all those people in San Diego who waited for a space ship to appear out of the sky and beam them up?

There was very little inviting about Frazier's house. The living room was oppressive. The wood floor was worn to a thin veneer and creaked as though unable to support a full-grown adult. The overhead fan clanged noisily against the ceiling, driving the temperature in the room further down. The house smelled of burnt popcorn and stale cigarette smoke.

Frazier obviously lived alone. The living room was so cluttered there was barely room for the dust to settle. The kitchen floor was lined with blotchy diamond patterned linoleum. His total assets weren't worth the price of a burger at McDonald's. Most of his meals were delivered once a day by the fellow over at the Meals on Wheels place and consisted of food he didn't particularly care for. He ate a few bites and fed the rest to the neighborhood cats.

Frazier attempted to stand upright. When his wobbly legs betrayed him, he plopped back into the chair. Determined, he propelled himself forward with a surge of force that almost sent him careening into the table.

"There," he said proudly. "No sonofabitching Cancer is going to keep me down." He reached for the metal walker, grabbed it firmly with both hands, and began to inch slowly toward the door. He barely squeaked across the doorjamb and slammed the screen door shut. He laughed, recalling the last time he'd been with a woman. She had said, "Don't let the door hit you in the ass on the way out." Seemed like lately that's all life had been doing. Hitting him in the ass.

His pace as pathetic as a turtle's, he alternated between dragging his legs and letting his arms do all the work. At other times he clicked into a rhythm of lift, drag, lift, drag until he reached the driver's side of the low slung 1964 Buick Electra convertible parked in the driveway. He wasn't quite sure where he was going, but he was sure he was headed somewhere. As he pulled out of the driveway, the engine purred like a fat kitten.

A newspaper clipping detailing Jemimah Hodge's recent appointment to the New Mexico State Police Forensics team stuck out of his jacket pocket. There was a reason Jerry Frazier wanted to see her—confession, redemption, call it what you will. *Jesus*, his life hadn't exactly been one a mother would be proud of, but this story needed to be told.

Those poor parents have suffered enough.

Chapter Eighteen

Jemimah glanced up from her desk as an elderly man on a walker tottered through the doorway. He was dressed in a wrinkled blue flannel warm-up suit and tattered sneakers. His hair was disheveled but it appeared he had expended some effort to clean himself up.

"How can I help you, Sir?" Jemimah said.

"Jerry Frazier. You can call me Jerry," he said.

"All right, Jerry. Have a seat. I'm a little busy, but perhaps I can point you in the right direction. Tell me what I can do for you."

"It's more along the line of what I can do for myself." He pulled the chair forward, knocking the aluminum walker to the floor.

Jemimah stepped toward him to retrieve the walker. Before she could reach it, he yanked it out of the way. "Sorry. I can handle it," he said stiffly.

She eased back in her swivel chair. "Of course, I was just ... do you mind if I take a few notes while we talk?" Jemimah opened the desk drawer and fumbled for a pen.

"No, not at all." He looked up at the clock on the wall. It was noon and he figured she was probably ready to go to lunch. He would make it quick.

"Okay, Jerry. What can I do for you?" she repeated. "I'm sorry. I must sound like a broken record."

His laugh was phlegmy. "That's all right. I tend to bring that out in people. Takes me a while to get going. You might want to take out one of them fancy tape recorders the detectives use on television, just in case."

Jemimah shifted in her chair as her stomach growled. She didn't want to seem too impatient. She wondered just what this man was hoping to accomplish by talking to her. Maybe he had a few traffic tickets he wanted fixed. Guess it wouldn't hurt to humor him until she figured out where she could send him. She reached into the desk drawer and pulled out a small cassette player, checked the battery and switched on the record button. She popped a piece of hard candy into her mouth to stave off the hunger pangs and offered one to Frazier. He declined with a wave of his hand, attempting to pull his chair forward to get comfortable.

"Mrs. Ilfeld didn't die in that wreck," Frazier blurted out.

Jemimah was thunderstruck. "Are you referring to Rose Ilfeld?"

"Yeah. The cop's wife. Came out in the paper about ten years ago that she had died in a wreck on the way to the hospital," he said. The air conditioning vent was blowing directly overhead. Frazier pulled his jacket around his shoulders and scooted his chair to one side.

"How did you know her, Jerry; was she a friend of yours?"

"Well, she used to call me every time she needed a little help in her garden. You know, moving rocks, digging holes, all the guy stuff. That husband of hers was too busy to do anything for her. She relied on me to do the heavy labor out in the yard. Things she couldn't do."

"How often did you help her?"

"Maybe a couple of times a month. It all depended on what she needed done. Sometimes she would just call out of the blue. Other times she would leave a note on my door, and I would show up at whatever time she said for me to be there."

Jemimah sensed that prying information out of Frazier

was going to be a challenge. She handed him a photo of Rose Ilfeld. "Is this the woman you're referring to?"

"Yep, that's her all right. She was a pretty lady, and nice, too. She never had a harsh word to say about anyone. Wasn't one to engage in petty gossip with the neighbors."

"Okay, so let's get serious here, Jerry. What is it you want to tell me? Are you here to make some kind of deal? Because if that's the case, I don't have much authority in that department."

Frazier looked perplexed and pulled his shoulders back, sitting erect. "No Ma'am. That's the furthest thing from my mind. I haven't committed any crime."

Jemimah noticed he was shaking, and reached out to put her hand over his. "I'm sorry. I had to ask. Don't be nervous, Jerry. You and I are the only ones privy to this conversation. Why don't you start at the beginning? Here, let me get you something to drink." Jemimah filled a glass at the water cooler and set it in front of him. He sipped it slowly.

"All right. About ten years ago around mid-June, I had gone back to finish up a small job for Mrs. Ilfeld. I wasn't supposed to go over there until the next day, but the weather was warm and perfect for setting up the cement. When I got there, I parked my truck in the alley so I could unload the bricks I had picked up at the Home Depot."

"How far is the alley from the house?"

"It's right in back, next to the fence, so it runs along the edge of the property line, perpendicular to the house. In the fifties and sixties the City used the alley for trash pickup and then they stopped. Modern trash trucks were too wide to fit between the fences. The residents use the alley when they want to unload stuff for their yards or haul trash away."

"So what did you do after you stacked the bricks?"

He wiped the sweat from his brow with his sleeve. "I figured I'd tell her I was there just in case she had changed her mind about where she wanted everything to go, you know?"

Jemimah nodded. "Continue."

"See, the front of the house runs parallel to the street. I mean, the long porch and the living room. Her garden is on the side of the house and stretches into the backyard. The front yard is mostly grass with a meandering brick pathway that runs from the back of the house to the front door. The alley runs east and west next to the side of the house where the garden is." He outlined a map on the top of the desk with his finger. "After I finished unloading and stacking the bricks, I walked up the pathway toward the house, minding my own business, intending to knock on the door to see if she was home. I could see her car in the driveway. I stopped when I heard someone arguing."

"How far away were you?"

"I was mostly behind a big lilac bush, maybe ten feet or so from the French doors."

"Could you hear what the argument was about?"

"The guy was hollering for her to shut up and she was crying hysterically, calling him a liar and a cheat. I could see them both from where I was standing but I don't think they could see me. As I said before, the living room faces the street and the French doors that open out to the porch were wide open."

Droplets of sweat were running down Frazier's face. Jemimah refilled his water glass. He pulled a handkerchief that had seen better days from his pocket and stopped to blow his nose. He wiped his face slowly and gulped a big swallow of water.

Jemimah took notes furiously in case the recorder decided to self-destruct in midstream. "And the man, did you recognize him?"

"I only met him once, but it was her husband, I'm pretty sure. His back was turned to me but she did say 'Damn you, Don, you've been seeing that slut all this time. How could you?' I could tell she was pretty upset, sounded like she'd been crying a lot. I sure did feel sorry for her. That was no way to treat a nice lady like Mrs. Ilfeld. She never did no wrong to anybody. She had a real nice disposition, always cheerful and stuff."

"What happened then?"

"I turned around and skedaddled back to my truck. Didn't want to get involved in no domestic disturbance. Been through enough of those on my own. Figured it wasn't a good time to announce my presence. Then I heard her scream. I ran back. It looked like he was choking her. She fell to the floor. He picked her up and put her on the couch."

Jerry stopped a moment, overcome with emotion. "It happened so fast, I don't know how long I stood there. There was nothing I could do to help her."

"So you just left?"

"This guy was a mean cop and I had a rap sheet a mile long. I wasn't about to hang around there and become a person of interest. I hightailed it back to my truck and jumped in. The damned thing wouldn't start." He looked up at Jemimah, his eyes huge with terror.

"What did you do then, Jerry?" Jemimah moved her chair next to his.

"While I was trying to figure out whether I should open the hood or not, I saw another State Police black and white drive up. The cop hurried into the house. I was watching through the cracks in the fence and praying like hell that they wouldn't see me. The trees in the yard blocked the alley but I still figured I'd be a dead man if they spotted me there." Frazier was becoming agitated as he relived the event.

"Let's stop for a minute, Jerry. Take a few sips of water and relax," she said.

"No, Ma'am. I'd rather just get it over with, if you don't mind."

"All right, but pace yourself. I can see this is very difficult for you to talk about. We can take a break anytime you feel the need."

"I been holding it in all these years, Ma'am. Never did have a reason to tell anyone about it," he said, his grip tightened on the arms of the chair.

"So tell me what else you saw after that," Jemimah checked to make sure the recording light was still flashing.

"As I said, I was watching through the gaps in the fence, waiting for the radiator on my truck to cool down enough so I could try to start it again. About ten minutes went by and then I saw the two cops carry Mrs. Ilfeld out of the house and put her in the passenger seat of the red car. The top was down and I could see they were trying to prop her up and she kept falling over, so they strapped her in with the seatbelt, I guess. Her husband got into the driver's seat and started the car up."

"What happened to the other officer; did you see where he went?"

"He got into his cruiser and took off. It looked to me like Mr. Ilfeld was pretending to have a conversation with her in the car, probably in case any neighbors were around, but I could see she was out like a light. She wasn't moving at all."

"Did you notice if there were any other people out and about in the neighborhood?"

"Oh, no. It was pretty quiet. I was scared shitless that either one of them would drive by and see me standing there in the alley. I got into my truck and crouched down. Good thing they went in the opposite direction, toward old Highway 85. My yellow truck stuck out like a sore thumb. No way they would have missed it."

"What happened after that, Jerry?"

"My truck finally kicked over and I got my ass out of there. I left town a couple of days later and didn't come back for a long time."

"How did you hear about Mrs. Ilfeld's accident?"

"Well, it's a bit complicated. I still had my little house on lower Alameda Street, so I decided things had probably cooled down enough to where I could come back, and besides, nobody had ever seen me in their neighborhood," he said. "We mostly worked in the side yard. People seemed to keep to their own business.

"So I returned to Santa Fe a few years ago and about a month later I read one of those memorial articles in the obituary section of the newspaper. It was the seventh anniversary of her passing, or something like that. You know, one of them fancy ads families put in the paper."

"One question, Mr. Frazier, Jerry. That second cop, the one that drove up to the house while you were watching from the alley, do you think you would recognize him if you saw him?"

"Well, it's been a long time, but maybe. He was tall and lanky and in uniform. But no, I was parked about half a block from the driveway. I guess not."

"All right, Jerry. I need to get your statement typed up. Would you be willing to sign it when that's done, to certify that this is what you saw?"

"Yes, Ma'am, I sure would. But I wouldn't take too long if I were you. As you might have noticed, I'm not planning on hanging around this world too much longer." His crooked smile revealed rows of tobacco-stained teeth. Jemimah saw a look of relief on his face. No doubt he was glad it was all over. She didn't want to appear too enthusiastic, but this chance meeting with Jerry Frazier might break the case wide open. Never in a million years did she think the solution would drop into her lap out of nowhere.

"Why don't I get my secretary on this right away? You can come back later this afternoon or you can wait right here."

Jemimah's initial skepticism had disappeared by the time Frazier had finished his story.

"If you don't mind, I'll just come back, Ma'am. These cop places give me the heebie-jeebies, if you know what I mean." He smiled another crooked smile.

"That will be fine." Jemimah reached out to shake his hand. "And Jerry, I want to thank you for coming forward. You don't know how much this is going to mean to the family."

"Yes. I think I do. It means a hell of a lot to me, too. Them poor folks. Thinking all these years that their daughter had died in an accident, when that mangy scoundrel killed her."

***

Frazier reached for his walker and dragged himself out to the hallway. He needed a smoke and a drink. He wound his way down the corridor to the exit. He stood for a moment and fumbled for his Salems. It was a task to manipulate the walker down the ramp while holding on to the pack of cigarettes and his lighter, so he stopped and lit up a few feet before he reached the door to the parking lot.

State Police Captain Jeff Whitney was making his way up the steps adjacent to the handicapped access ramp. Jerry Frazier gave him a long, hard look and took a drag of his cigarette. Whitney returned the stare.

"Hey, old geezer, didn't you see the No Smoking signs?"

Chapter Nineteen

Katie Gonzales was an experienced legal assistant assigned by the Department to Jemimah's office. She was thirty-something, attractive to a fault, and a confirmed date-aholic. She wore tight-fitting tops that showed off her ample chest and kept her dark brown hair cut in a short bob. She worked at the Sheriff's complex each Friday, processing Jemimah's reports and creating both paper and computer case files.

Jemimah was impressed by Katie's ability to accomplish so much work while she chewed gum, talked on the phone, and flirted with almost every male who wandered within twenty feet of her desk.

"I don't know how I ever kept anything in order without you, Katie. And you manage to accomplish it all in just one day a week," Jemimah said.

Katie grinned. "I love working for you, Dr. Hodge. I look forward to Fridays. You're involved in such fascinating cases. Nothing boring about your job."

"Seems that way lately, but I can assure you that I do work on cases that can be pretty dull, particularly those cases where the suspect's behavior is over the top and there's no way anyone is going to get him to confess, not even the best of detectives."

"Speaking of detectives, how are things going with you and the Lieutenant? Are you two dating yet?" Katie smiled.

Jemimah laughed. "Why do you ask? Detective Romero and I are just working associates."

"That's not what I've heard. According to Clarissa, he's only got eyes for you."

"Didn't I hear that in a song? I trust you don't put a lot of stock in Clarissa's gossip." Jem chuckled. "But really, we are just friends," Jemimah wasn't sure whether she was trying to convince Katie or herself.

Katie rolled her eyes. "Bummer."

Jemimah glanced at her watch. "Not to change the subject, Katie, but I have a meeting in twenty minutes on the other side of town. Do you mind finishing that Frazier statement? He's scheduled to come by later today. I should be back by then. He won't be hard to miss. Gray-haired guy on a walker."

"Sure," Katie bubbled. "Be glad to. I'll leave it on your desk."

Jemimah retrieved her briefcase and hurried out. She had a near collision with Captain Whitney as she rushed around the corner. She could have sworn he glared at her as he grunted a hello, but with his trademark darker than night sunglasses, it was difficult to tell. She didn't bother to exchange pleasantries and just remarked, "Good day, Whit."

Her meeting lasted longer than expected. Traffic on St. Francis Drive and the bypass was heavier than usual. She parked in her assigned space and climbed the stairs two at a time. She was winded by the time she walked into her office.

Katie looked up. "Well, hello again, Doc. I was just getting ready to call it a day. Wasn't sure you were going to make it back before five. Thought you might have stopped at Los Angelos for happy hour."

"Nothing doing. Too many sharks swimming around the bar this time of day," Jemimah said. "Katie, by chance did Jerry Frazier come by to sign the affidavit?"

"No, he didn't. I took a few minutes break down the hall but I would have seen him if he'd come in. You mentioned he was on a walker and nobody fitting that description came by. The file's on your desk."

Jemimah was bewildered. It was nearing five o'clock and the main doors to the complex would be closing shortly. She slid the file into her briefcase and resolved to stop by Frazier's house on Saturday.

Katie finished up her day with a final look in her compact to apply a fresh coat of fire-engine red lipstick. "Anything else you need before I take off, Doc?"

"Not a thing, Katie. Thank you."

"Then I'll see you next Friday. Sure you don't want to join me for a quick drink to chill down?"

"I'm sure, Katie. Full moon tonight, so be careful out there."

"My horoscope says I'm going to meet someone tall, dark and handsome."

"That could be a vampire, you think?"

"I always carry a silver cross in my purse, just in case." Katie waved goodnight and headed out the door, quickly falling in step with one of the rookie detectives walking toward the parking lot.

Jemimah wasn't in a hurry to enter late afternoon traffic. She waited until the parking lot of the corrections facility across the street emptied out before she fetched her belongings and made her way out to her vehicle. She'd been on duty since early that morning and high on her list right now was a hot bath, a leisurely dinner and a glass of Chardonnay.

Out in the parking lot, she started up her car, buckled up and pulled onto the almost deserted highway. The radio was tuned to a classical music station playing a sleepy violin concerto. She popped in a CD and drove the remainder of the distance home listening to Creedence Clearwater Revival, music that always managed to put her in a cheerful mood.

Chapter Twenty

State Police officer Jeff Whitney was having a bad day and trying to shake it off. He'd spent the morning at the National Guard qualifying range, watching State Police Academy rookies handle their weapons like ten-year-olds. Most would fail the proficiency requirements and it was going to reflect on him. He parked his cruiser in his assigned space at State Police Headquarters on the south end of Cerrillos Road and trudged down the hallway to his office. Tossing his briefcase on the couch, he checked his messages.

Shortly before noon, he peeked through the door of Police Chief Suazo's office and ambled over to Patsy Lujan's desk in an office adjacent to the secretarial pool. Although Patsy considered herself a tad on the abundant side, she wore her clothes well. Her long leather boots and short skirt accentuated her muscular legs. A nice rack squeezing through the edges of her tank top garnered her a few extra points on Whitney's scale. Hell, he wasn't going to marry her, he was just going to poke around for information, and if he had to sleep with her, he could deal with that. At least she wasn't so butt ugly he'd have to cover her face.

"Miss Patsy, you get prettier every day," Whitney drawled as he removed his hat and sunglasses in a well-choreographed movement. He smiled his most seductive smile and licked his lips for added effect, a technique he had perfected over many years of flirting with women, whether he was interested or not.

Patsy blushed, fanned herself with a file folder and flashed him a big smile. "Oh, *Cap-ten* Whitney, you say that to all the girls. I've heard you."

She spoke with a strong Spanish accent that seemed to pop up when least expected, and it reminded him of Speedy Gonzales, *the fastest raton in all of* Me-hi-co.

"Only to the pretty ones, Patsy. That turquoise color sure looks nice on you. Brings out your eyes." He bent toward her, his nose almost touching hers.

"Stop, already," she chortled. "What can I do for you? The Chief's out until next *Fry-dee*."

"Didn't come to see the Chief, pretty lady. Thought we might catch a bite to eat tonight, maybe a movie? I know it's awfully short notice. New restaurant opened up at the Railyard. They say the steaks are pretty good."

Patsy looked surprised. "*We*, as in you and me?" She giggled.

"Of course I mean you. You're the prettiest lady in the room. That is, unless you have other plans?" Whitney knew he was bending the rules about dating hired help, but he wasn't going on a date. He was on a mission.

"Well?" he added, a sly grin on his face, "What do you think?"

"Oh sure, I guess. Yeah, that would be n-nice," Patsy stammered.

"Pick you up at seven?" He smiled again.

"Yes, of course," she said, handing him a slip of paper with her address and cell number.

"See you later, Sweetie." He winked.

Patsy let out a contented sigh and reshuffled the papers on her desk.

Whitney walked out to the parking lot and sat in his squad car for a few minutes. He turned the key in the ignition and pressed the a/c button. Out of habit, he opened both side windows and dusted off the dashboard with a dust rag.

Reaching for his phone, he dialed Patsy's number: "Hey, sweet thing. Change of plans. Something just came up this second."

Patsy's voice faded with disappointment. "Oh, sure, what is it?"

"Can we just meet at the bar in the restaurant? I know that's a lot to ask of you, but—"

Before he could finish the sentence, she blurted, "Oh, yes, of course. I'll see you there."

Whitney was a conniver. No use raising Patsy's hopes for a second date by picking her up at her house. He knew she came from an established Santa Fe family and probably had one of those *Pachuco* fathers who showed every guy who dated his daughter his tattoos and his weapons collection. Besides, he was twice her age and maybe as old as her father. Whitney had managed to play the field longer than he would have dreamed possible, but he wasn't about to tempt the Fates. The force was full of guys his age who hooked up with younger women and Bam! Ended up with another round of kids to add to the ones grown and on their own.

No way, José.

He had his master plan mapped out and it didn't include knocking up a twenty-something, starry eyed *Chicana* girl. His plan involved early retirement and never having to worry about finances—or blackmailers—again.

At 7:05 that evening, Whitney saw Patsy sitting at the bar, glancing nervously toward the door. Judging from her slightly glazed appearance, she was on her second or third drink, something sweet—a double Amaretto Sour or a pomegranate margarita. She must have arrived early. She wore a figure-hugging short dress and strappy black heels. She looked again as Whitney came through the door, sans sunglasses and police uniform. She licked her lips. She was practically drooling, he noted.

The bar was crowded, music blaring over the speakers. It wasn't Whitney's type of music, no guitars twanging in the background. Customers mingled at the bar, waiting to pounce on a stool the moment someone even intimated they were about to leave. Whitney took a quick detour, stopped by a table to give the buxom blonde a quick embrace and scanned the bar. He let out a whistle as he approached Patsy.

"Wow, is that you, Miss Patsy?" He hated sounding like the character from *Driving Miss Daisy,* but it suited the role he liked to play—a cross between Clark Gable and Sean Connery.

Patsy gave a throaty laugh, already a little too loud. She didn't seem to mind that he was a late. Perhaps she was just relieved he hadn't stood her up.

"Officer Whitney, you're funny!" But her look said that he looked hot and she'd like to suggest they go somewhere and screw each other's brains out.

"It's after five, Patsy. Call me Jeff."

Whitney gave her the once-over. He was going to enjoy this "date" a lot more than he'd anticipated. Every guy in the bar was looking at her with their tongues hanging out.

"You're real pretty tonight, Patsy. I feel a little underdressed," he declared as he slid onto the stool next to hers.

"Oh, you look great, Jeff. You know how casual the restaurants around here are." He knew he filled out his black Wranglers and red t-shirt pretty well. The alligator boots added another couple of inches to his already tall frame.

Whitney was fully aware of the impression he made on women of all ages. He saw how they checked him out at the gym, standing in line at the grocery store, and as he strolled through police headquarters.

"Do you mind if we move to a booth, Patsy? Our table won't be ready for another half hour." He motioned the bartender to refill her drink and ordered a Scotch on the rocks as he guided her toward a dimly lit booth. It was noticeably quieter there. At least they didn't have to holler over the crowd gathered around the bar.

"So, Patsy, how did you get so pretty?" he teased, moving closer for full effect.

She laughed and fluttered her lashes. "I don't know how to answer that."

Whitney gently slid the cocktail toward her and chugged half of his in one gulp. "It doesn't require an answer, Honey. Just my way of telling you again how hot you look tonight. Not that you don't always look great." He smiled and touched her knee.

Her saw her melt a little as she lifted the drink to her lips and almost dropped the glass.

"Sorry, I didn't mean to embarrass you. Tell me a little about yourself. Did you grow up in Santa Fe?"

A few drinks later, their table was ready and the hostess arrived to lead the way. Whitney, who was involved in a long wet kiss with Patsy, had kept one eye open. He motioned with his free arm for her to get lost. He was moving in on Patsy and he wasn't even going to be required to spring for dinner.

Out in the parking lot, he opened the passenger side door, hopped around to the driver's side and slid under the steering wheel.

"Nice car."

He leaned over, put his hand under her chin and pulled her toward him. He clicked on the ignition and headed the vehicle around the parking lot to the exit. She was ripe for the picking. He reached over and grasped her hand. By the time they arrived at the motel, the car windows were covered with steam. He'd kept his arm around her the entire drive and had kissed her hungrily at six of the seven traffic lights. After breezing through the check-in at the Chamisa Inn, he retrieved the room key and slid the car into the space in front of the door.

A few seconds after sliding the keycard into the slot of a

corner room, most of their clothes were scattered on the floor.

CR

At three o'clock in the morning. Whitney brushed his teeth and slid back into bed. Patsy moaned, complaining about the light in her eyes.

"So sorry, Sweetie. Had to get up—too much to drink," he lied. "Go back to sleep. I'll be all right. I can flip through this magazine until I get sleepy again."

"No, no. I'm awake," she whispered. He could see that she was still pretty wasted. Her eyes were mostly closed and she struggled to keep them open.

Perfect.

He leaned over and gently kissed her eyes, one at a time. "Patsy, honey, tell me about your boss. When's he coming back?"

"Hmmm, oh, I don't know. Next week. Next day. Tomorrow," she slurred.

Whitney brushed a wisp of hair from her cheek. "So what's this big hush-hush case I've been hearing so much about?"

She turned over on her side. Whitney gently rolled her over to him. He kissed her neck, her breasts, and her lips. That calculated move served to wake her up a bit. He repeated the question.

"Mmmm, which one?"

"You know, the one everyone in the Department whispers about but nobody claims to know anything about." He faked a chuckle. His lips brushed her navel. She groaned. "Come on, Patsy, you know what I'm talking about. Focus."

She couldn't help herself. She was becoming more aroused.

"Tell me, Sweetie. Then you can have it again."

She squirmed. He blew a puff of smoke toward her. He passed her the joint, and a few deep drags loosened her tongue considerably as he continued his slow and deliberate southward journey.

"You mean the case that forensic lady is working on? That's the only hush-shush ...."

Whitney's ears perked up. "Yeah, yeah," he said in a low, seductive voice. "Tell me about it."

"All I know is some case about an officer's dead wife. Old case from way back. Nobody knows she has it. Suazo wasn't chief yet. Only he and a few people know about it."

"And?" he prodded, concentrating on the curve of her belly.

"Ohhh, I don't know. Found some old guy who witnessed the whole thing. She's waiting for him to come in and sign a statement." Patsy moaned audibly. "Can we stop talking now? It hurts my ears."

"Does this old dude have a name, Honey?" he said.

"Gary ... Jerry … Frazier, something like that." She was starting to sound cranky.

Whitney was done prodding. He gave her a few extra thrusts for good measure and finished with a flourish. She'd have a lot to write in her Dear Diary, but he was confident she wouldn't remember anything but the sex. By the time he rolled over on his side to catch a few hours of shut-eye, she was out like a light, a Mona Lisa smile on her face.

So, there had been a witness after all. Why had Whitney gotten involved in all of this to begin with? What a mess. Oh, yeah, he'd hated to see his drinking buddy and wingman Don Ilfeld domesticated, and the guy had been pretty hard-up for cash—some gambling debt he couldn't tell his wife about, a wife who'd quickly turned into a bore after the wedding, especially when she'd discovered he was cheating. Don felt pretty confident about eliciting his ol' friend Whitney's aid; they'd shared a lot, especially that time Ilfeld had seen Whitney help himself to some of the money they'd picked up during drug busts.

Hell, it wasn't even that much money. Just a little

skimmed off the top. $5,000 or so … at least that was all Don knew about. Money no one would miss. Don had asked nothing in return for his silence, until that day he strangled his wife "accidentally."

It had been an accident of sorts, but he owed Don big time. And Don never would have convinced anyone he didn't mean to strangle his wife during that argument, not with all those gambling debts and the big insurance payout he stood to receive. Who else would they point the finger at? After all, the husband was always the suspect, right? But then, Don had been lying about her health, trying to explain her absence at various events. She'd stayed home because she knew he was cheating on her.

How to explain her injuries, leading to her death ….

Don had told everyone that she had chronic leukemia. What if she had needed to go to the hospital in a hurry, and he was injured during the drive …. She'd be thrown from the vehicle and killed. All Whitney would have to do was turn a blind eye.

But hell, even a blind man could see that Don had messed up. No wonder that EMT had been suspicious. Luckily the man had given up telling the precinct about his suspicions after a while—but the family had continued to ask questions. And now almost ten years had gone by and he was almost home free …. *Almost*.

And then there was Romero. He'd been convinced that the guy was in on the investigation somehow. Even went to some trouble to get rid of him. But the guy had nine lives. He should have taken better aim.

By five thirty that morning, Whitney was showered and dressed. He reached into his pocket and dropped a few bills on the night table. He left an unsigned note:

> Patsy, Sweetie. Stay a while. Have some breakfast. Catch a cab back to your car. Duty calls.
> XOXO

Chapter Twenty-One

Cooler than usual nighttime breezes heralded summer's approaching farewell. But it was Santa Fe, and it was never over until it was over. Around eight thirty that evening, raindrops tapped a flamenco rhythm on the roof of Tim McCabe's massive adobe house. He nodded off to sleep halfway through a *Rawhide* rerun. An hour later the ringing phone broke Laura's focus as she thumbed through Richard McGarrity's latest mystery.

She nudged her husband gently. "The phone's on your side, dear."

McCabe opened one eye, pulling himself up on the pillow. He reached for the phone. "McCabe here," he said.

It was Detective Romero. "Tim, sorry to ring you so late at night."

"S'alright," McCabe said. "We're still up, what's going on?"

"We have a situation," Laura heard Romero tell her husband. The phone's volume was turned way up. "I just got a call from the nine-one-one dispatcher. Some guy's laid out in the middle of a field near the Rodeo Grounds. Possible homicide. I don't have much info yet."

"What do you need me to do, Rick?" McCabe asked, a little more awake.

"I'm a bit shorthanded. Most of the troops are at a seminar in Albuquerque. Any chance you can meet me at the County fairgrounds?"

McCabe sat upright. "Sure. I can do that. I'll be there as fast as I can."

McCabe pulled on his jeans and jumped into his boots. He leaned over and kissed Laura lightly on the cheek as he buttoned his shirt. "Honey, I'm sorry. That was Detective Romero. He's a little shorthanded. I have to go. I'll call you first chance I get."

Laura McCabe reached for the TV remote. It was going to be another long night. She was beginning to regret the feigned enthusiasm she expressed when her husband first told her of the Sheriff's efforts to get him appointed to the post of Special Investigator. Even though it had begun as a part-time assignment, her husband was spending more time playing Sherlock Holmes than he was taking care of business. She felt like having a stiff drink. Instead she listened to a sermon by Joel Osteen, the latest wonder-boy on the televangelical circuit, who with an engaging smile and beaming countenance assured her and the thirty thousand people in the stadium that God would be rewarding them with great abundance for their steadfastness. She wondered what had become of the Crystal Cathedral of years past, and did she really care?

⊂⊇

Tim McCabe thrust his arm out the window of the Hummer and secured the flashing blue light onto its roof. For a Saturday night, there was little traffic on the main roads. The UNM Lobo basketball team was hosting an exhibition game in The Pit and many Santa Fe fans had headed toward Albuquerque in the early hours of the afternoon to crowd into Lobo Stadium. As he sped toward Rodeo Road, McCabe listened to the sportscaster describe the final minutes of a very close game. Just up ahead the flashing lights of Lieutenant Romero's car caught his attention. Ambulance lights blinked in the distance behind them. Both McCabe and Detective

Romero drove toward a man frantically waving his arms.

"This way," the man hollered. "Over here."

"All right, sir," Romero said, alighting from his cruiser. "What's going on?"

Peter Bertram reached out to shake Romero's hand and introduce himself. He filled them in on how he discovered the body, although at the time it was not yet a dead body.

"There's a guy in the field over there. I was out walking my dogs, two chows, when they started pulling on their leashes and barking their heads off. We almost tripped over him. I didn't know if he was dead or alive. I didn't want to go near him. My dogs were going crazy, so I took them home and came back in my car. Took you guys long enough to get here." Bertram was a stocky man in his late twenties. He appeared angry and agitated.

Romero reminded him that it had only been twenty minutes since the 9-1-1 call was forwarded to him. "How long did it take you to get your dogs back home and pick up your car?"

"I dunno. Maybe fifteen minutes, maybe more," Bertram said. "It was just starting to get dark."

"Just stay right here, Mr. Bertram. I'll come back for your statement as soon as we check things out. McCabe, help me with this light."

McCabe beamed the light toward the field to direct the ambulance driver to the scene. Romero ran to the victim's side. The field was still wet from a recent rain and mud sloshed up to his ankles.

The victim was a gray-haired man dressed in what appeared to be navy blue flannel pajamas. He was face down in the murky field, dead or unconscious. Either way, he wasn't moving. A few feet away, an aluminum walker lay tipped over on its side. His clothes and what Romero could see of his body were covered with mud. As he flashed the light over the victim, he saw an open wound on the side of his head. Romero checked for a pulse. He thought he felt a faint heartbeat, *or did he?* He couldn't be sure. He waved the EMTs in his direction. The two ambulance techs rushed forward, lugging their equipment through the bog.

Roger Streeter, recently promoted to head EMT for the County, slapped an oxygen mask over the man's face.

"Damn," Streeter said. "The mud out here is pretty deep. It's going to be a bitch to get him into the ambulance."

"Do what you can. We need to get him out of here, soon," Romero said curtly. "The rain's starting up again. We'll help you carry the gurney if need be. Let me know when you're ready."

Romero trudged over to Bertram the witness, who now sat in his car. He rolled down the window as Romero approached.

"You thinking maybe the guy might have taken a nasty fall? What would compel that dude to try maneuvering a walker across this field of mud? Is he nuts, or what?" Bertram asked, looking straight at Romero.

"I'm not sure it's that cut and dried, Mr. Bertram."

"You think maybe someone was trying to kill him?"

Romero's voice had an edge. It took all he had to keep from smacking this insensitive excuse for a human being. "Too early to say."

"Hey, I was just making conversation. I've been standing around here in the rain waiting. My dinner's getting cold," Bertram whined.

Romero tried to keep his anger in check. "What I can't understand, Sir, is why you didn't bother to see if the man was breathing before you decided to go home, drop the dogs off and pick up your car. Right now I'm not sure he has a rat's chance in hell of making it, if he's even alive."

"Hey, I'm not my brother's keeper," Bertram snapped. "At least I took my dogs home and came back in my car to call you guys. I could have just let some other Good Samaritan find him tomorrow."

Romero spit into the mud. "You could also have called nine-one-one before you did that."

McCabe had donned latex gloves and was scouting the area for anything suspicious. "If there was any evidence around here, the mud has swallowed it up."

"McCabe, walk this Good Samaritan over to the cruiser and take his statement." He hurried back to the EMTs, who had placed the victim on the stretcher. Romero guided them across the mud to the ambulance.

"Any ID on this guy?" Romero said.

"Yeah," said Streeter. "Here's his wallet."

Romero ran his light over the contents: Jerry Frazier, 204 Alameda Street, Santa Fe, NM. 62. He handed the wallet to McCabe, who placed it in an evidence bag.

Detective Arthur Chacon and the crime techs drove onto the scene as the ambulance departed. While the techs gathered their equipment, Artie walked over to Romero and shook his hand. "Hey, Boss. What we got here?"

"So far we've got a victim already half-dead when the EMTs arrived. His wallet was still on him. Doesn't look like robbery to me. There were six undisturbed one dollar bills. He was discovered by a guy walking his dogs who took about half an hour to run home, leave the dogs and get back here to call nine-one-one. Might as well treat it like a crime scene," Romero said as he turned toward his cruiser. McCabe fell in step with him.

"Too bad the rain made such a mess of everything around here," McCabe said.

"You know, for the life of me I can't figure out what a guy on a walker was doing out here in the middle of the field," Romero said.

"Does he live in this area?"

"Nope. Down on Alameda Street somewhere. Not too far from the Plaza, according to the address," Romero said.

"That's about eleven miles away. If he drove here, there'd

at least be a vehicle nearby. I took a look around. The nearest place is the Chavez Center and that's been closed since six o'clock. Nobody in the parking lot but security. There's only a workout center around here, and from the looks of the walker, doubt if he was doing that," McCabe said.

"I'm thinking maybe he was dumped," Romero said. "They threw the walker in to make it appear he was at this location to begin with."

"Well if he was, everything viable's sure been washed away by now."

Romero pulled out next to Detective Chacon. "See what you can find."

"Will do, Lieutenant," Chacon said.

"McCabe and I will be at the hospital on the off-chance the guy survives and can give a statement when he's stable."

McCabe started up his vehicle. Persistent drops continued to fall at a steady pace. The scene was pitch black except for the narrow illumination of their flashlights. "I'll meet you at the hospital," Romero heard him shout.

"Okay, Tim. Right behind you."

The drive to Santa Fe's only hospital took ten minutes, windshield wipers operating at top speed in the relentless rain. Romero and McCabe entered the waiting room together. The orderly at the front desk directed them to a section in the rear corner of the ER. Romero flashed his credentials and hurried to the victim's bedside, where a young nurse's aide was busy wiping dirt from Jerry Frazier's face and body. His muddy clothing was piled in the metal basket next to the bed.

"Oh, you can't come back here, Sir. Family only," the aide said.

Romero flashed his badge again. He was beginning to think cops should wear big metal stars on their chest pockets with the word SHERIFF imprinted on them, just like in the spaghetti westerns on TV.

"Sorry," she said. "I'm new here. I don't know any of the

police officers who come in here regularly."

Romero forced a weak smile. "Yes, I understand. Can we speak to the doctor in charge?"

"Oh, this guy doesn't need a doctor. He's dead, you know. I'm just cleaning him up while they try to find his family."

It appeared to Romero that she was holding back tears as she continued to lovingly wipe the man's forehead.

He asked her gently, "Miss, would you direct me to the doctor who saw Mr. Frazier when he was brought into the Emergency Room?"

"Oh," she smiled. "That would be Doctor Hillyer. Amos Hillyer. He's brilliant."

"Yes, I know who he is. Do you think you can get someone to page him?" Romero asked.

"Oh, no, Sir." She hesitated. "My supervisor said for me to stay right here and clean this mess up. I don't know why they can't just give him a bath."

Romero figured the victim was the first dead person this young lady had seen in her short career as a nurse's aide, an experience they surely didn't offer as part of the curriculum at the local Community College.

"I'll take the heat for sending you off, Miss. Janet, is it?" Romero smiled.

"Yes," she sighed. "Janet Garcia. Certified Nurse's Aide," she pointed to her name tag. "This is my first job," she added nervously.

"Janet, everything is fine. Take a sip of water, relax a minute, and then please have someone page Dr. Hillyer," McCabe said. He watched as the young girl walked down the hall, her pony tail bobbing with every step. "I feel sorry for some of these young kids. Looks like she belongs at a receptionist desk rather than back here caretaking the dead and dying."

"Amen," said Romero. "Or she might be one of those

who actually make it, a hundred bodies later."

Dr. Hillyer walked in at the tail end of the conversation.

"Like doctors, good nurses are cultivated by being in the middle of real-life situations. That young lady just experienced something not found in a textbook. She's going to be just fine.

"What can I do for you gentlemen? I have a very busy ER tonight," he said. "I can only spare a few minutes before the backlog turns into a revolt."

The detective and his sidekick looked up at the distinguished doctor. Romero shook his hand and introduced McCabe.

"You might not remember me, Mr. McCabe. We've attended a few social functions together. Our wives know each other. And I've had the pleasure of sewing both you men up. You last year in the spring, and the Lieutenant here about a month ago." Dr. Hillyer smiled broadly.

McCabe gave his hand a vigorous shake. "I do remember, indeed, Sir. At least we meet this time under better circumstances. Neither of us needing to be sewn up or patched together."

"How's that shoulder coming along, Detective—can I assume you've followed up with your doctor?"

"Still in some pain, Doc, but getting better. Ibuprofen helps."

"What can I do for you? I know you're not here on a social visit," Dr. Hillyer said.

"What's the verdict on Mr. Frazier here?" Romero said. "I was hoping we could have asked a few questions before he passed on."

"Unfortunately, he was DOA. The EMT said he detected a very faint pulse at the site, but nothing more once they put him in the ambulance. But I am familiar with Mr. Frazier. I've seen him in the ER a couple of times in the past year. Could have saved your criminal the trouble of committing such a heinous act on such a sick man," Dr. Hillyer said.

"How so?" Romero said.

"He never had a chance. Mr. Frazier suffered from terminal Cancer which had metastasized to most of his body. He would have probably died within a month or so anyway," said Dr. Hillyer. "He was being treated at the hospital's cancer center, but there was nothing more they could do. He was as terminal as one can get. His organs were methodically shutting down and it was just a matter of time. But he was a tough old coot."

"So did he die from his injuries?"

"Well, my educated guess is that Mr. Frazier died of suffocation from being face down in the mud for an extended period of time. The X-rays showed a lot of residue in his lungs and bronchi and that tells me he was probably alive when his face hit the ground. He was barely alive when they put him in the ambulance. Even if he had survived, he would have been a vegetable. Blunt force trauma, I suppose. Whoever it was hit him pretty hard from behind. He never felt a thing. Knocked most of his brains out. But since I'm not the Coroner, our conversation doesn't go beyond this room." Hillyer paused and made a few notes on Frazier's chart.

"Thanks, Doc. I appreciate the info. I assume your staff has already contacted our esteemed Coroner?" Romero said.

"Indeed we have. I placed the call myself right before I came in here."

McCabe suspected the young Amos Hillyer would have made a fine detective before he morphed into old Dr. Hillyer, the renowned emergency room surgeon. It was almost three in the morning. Romero went home to catch a few hours' sleep. McCabe, on the other hand, drove home with only one thing on his mind—how he was going to make it up to Laura this time.

Chapter Twenty-Two

Jemimah dressed in a hurry that morning, already late for a meeting with Lieutenant Romero. She was awakened at five o'clock by the incessant yelping of her Border Collie out in the yard, followed by frantic scratching at the screen door. Barely awake, she plodded her way across the cold Saltillo tile floor and opened the front door, expecting the dog to jump all over her with customary early morning affection. Instead Jemimah was overcome by the unmistakable foul odor of skunk. Molly rolled on the carpet and rubbed her eyes with her paws. Three hours had elapsed by the time Jemimah rounded up the miserable dog and bathed her in every remedy she could find, including baking soda and peroxide.

She grabbed her stack of files, shoved them in the satchel, and headed out the door as the dog snoozed on the couch, oblivious to anything but its own comfort. Jemimah arrived at Romero's office in record time. Fortunately she lived only five miles from the substation in Cerrillos. Clarissa gave her a fond embrace as she entered the office.

"Jemimah, how great to see you. You look wonderful. Love the streaks in your hair," she tittered.

"Thanks, Clarissa. One bottle of Clairol and twenty minutes," she smiled, recalling how twenty minutes had stretched to over an hour. Next time she'd definitely see a hairdresser.

"Well, whatever you did, girl, it looks good on you," Clarissa gushed.

"Is your esteemed boss in his office?"

"He's expecting you. Go right in," Clarissa continued to percolate.

QR

Romero sat at his desk engrossed in a case file. She tapped on the doorway. He looked up and smiled.

"Hey, Jemimah. Good to see you. Come in, come in. Have a seat. Just need to read these last few sentences." What he really wanted to do was put the file down and spend a few minutes looking at her. A smile crossed his face as Tim McCabe's advice came to mind. Give her some room. She'll come around. He closed the file folder and placed it in the drawer.

"Well, Jem. Long time no see. Sorry I wasn't able to make our last two appointments, but I'm all yours now," he beamed. "So how can I help you?"

Jemimah looked surprised. She was silent for a moment before she said, "How are you, Rick? How is your shoulder?"

"Better," he said, "I have to keep reminding myself not to make any sudden movements. But enough about me. Bring me up to speed on your case, Jem. Is there anything I can help you with? Maybe open a few doors, call in a few favors?"

He could see that he'd thrown her off balance. She definitely wasn't used to his being so affable. She gave herself a little shake before continuing, as if reminding herself to concentrate.

"In a nutshell," she replied, "I've been dissecting the Ilfeld case file every spare chance I get. There's not a heck of a lot of strong evidence in there to pinpoint the cause of Rose Ilfeld's death as a homicide. Just the suspicions of the parents and siblings that maybe Officer Ilfeld wanted his wife dead for the insurance money. According to the mother, he had a gambling habit and was in pretty deep with his bookies and afraid that his wife was going to find out about it."

"Were you able to interview any ex-wives or girlfriends? Sometimes they have a lot to say after the relationship has broken up." He was genuinely interested in helping her move the case forward.

"I found one ex-girlfriend, Kitty Legits, but she wouldn't admit to dating him while he was still married. I had the distinct impression that she was still seeing him on occasion. She seemed to have kept up with his comings and goings."

Clarissa poked her head in the door. "Excuse me, Boss. Coroner's report you were waiting for on that Frazier fellow just faxed in. Blunt force trauma," she said.

"Thank you, Clarissa. Fax a copy off to Detective Chacon. I've assigned the investigation to him."

Jemimah raised her hand in a "stop" motion. "Hold on a minute, Rick. Frazier. What's the guy's first name?"

Romero glanced at her while he skimmed down the two-page report he'd been compiling. "Ah, here it is. Frazier. Jerry Frazier, Age sixty-two. Guess it was a homicide after all. The ER doc was right on. At first I thought maybe the guy had just gotten caught in the rain, but when we arrived at the hospital, Dr. Hillyer expressed the opinion that he had been hit from behind."

Jemimah gasped. Romero looked up to see the color drain from her face.

"Hey, are you all right? What's going on, Jem?"

"Oh crap, Rick. I've been working so damned hard on this Ilfeld case and now it's gone all to hell."

"What are you talking about, Jem. What does this dead guy have to do with your case?"

Jemimah quickly gained her composure. "It's a complicated story. Jerry Frazier showed up at my office out of nowhere a few days ago and told me a bizarre story about this case. He apparently had witnessed the murder of Rose Ilfeld. He was supposed to come back later in the day to sign the statement he gave me, but he never show up. I thought maybe he was under the weather or something. I knew he wasn't a well man. I planned to stop by his house later today and get him to sign it. I don't believe this is happening."

"This puts a whole new spin on the investigation. Instead of just being random, the mugging may just tie into the Ilfeld case. Damn. And the crime scene was so muddy we weren't able to collect a single shred of evidence."

"Does that mean his statement isn't going to be worth the paper it's written on?"

"Jem, let me ask you this. By chance did you record Frazier's statement?"

"Yes, since I didn't really know his reason for coming to see me, I was just going to take down a few notes, and then he suggested I record it, so I did. Why do you ask?"

"I know you're not a seasoned investigator, and it's probably not part of your job description, but as long as you asked his name and address, something to prove that it was Frazier who was giving the statement. That would probably hold up in any court."

Jemimah breathed a sigh of relief. "Oh, I sure hope so."

"Let's get back to the synopsis you were giving me. You indicated you've interviewed a few of Ilfeld's old girlfriends and acquaintances."

"Yes, but that didn't produce much in the way of evidence. Just more confirmation that Ilfeld had been stepping out on his wife, which in today's society doesn't seem to be a crime," she said. "Presidents do it, politicians do it, and cops do it."

"Have you interviewed any of his friends on the force?"

"Are you kidding? Chief Suazo won't allow me to go there. Anyone I make an effort to contact would probably run straight to Ilfeld and alert him that I'm snooping around. This is all supposed to be highly confidential."

"Of course that leaves pretty boy Whitney out of the loop, too," he said. Romero suppressed the impulse to say something snide about him.

"There's a lot more to this case than meets the eye, Rick. I think there's another State Police officer involved, not only in the cover-up but in the actual incident. Coincidentally, his partner at the time was—"

Before she could finish her sentence, Clarissa poked her head in the door again. "Sorry, Boss. But the Sheriff's waiting for you outside in his cruiser. Seems you two have an appointment somewhere? He's tapping his fingers on the dash and he said to hurry it up."

"Oh, Jeez. Tell him I'll be right there. Jemimah, I'm sorry. Medrano called me at six o'clock this morning to set up this surveillance. He said it would be spur of the moment. We'll have to continue our conversation another time. Can I call you first chance I get?"

"Yes, of course. You have my cell number," she said, gathering her files.

Romero gathered his weapon and ammo and walked with her to the parking lot. As he guided her through the door, he touched the small of her back lightly. He noticed she didn't flinch.

Chapter Twenty-Three

It was a balmy August day, perfect for picking apples. The heat was barely noticeable as a pleasant breeze crisscrossed through the air, cooling things down a notch in the shaded back yard. Tim McCabe had put off this task far longer than usual. It wasn't as though he couldn't hire a few Mexican day workers from the park downtown to do the harvesting. He just preferred to do himself. Maybe it was because it took him back to his childhood on the family ranch in Idaho where each year a few apple trees provided a bumper crop. Or maybe this was the one way he could be close to nature. These days business at the gallery and his work load at the Sheriff's Department took up more and more of his leisure hours. The task also provided an opportunity for him to spend a little quality time with Laura, who seemed to be a bit preoccupied these days.

McCabe's schedule was clear for the next two days and he was looking forward to getting started. It was nine o'clock by the time the couple finished a leisurely breakfast out on the patio. He and Laura gathered baskets from the shed and stacked them on the motorized cart. McCabe maneuvered the small tractor through the yard and loaded up two stepladders outfitted with containers to hold the harvested fruit.

"This is great, isn't it Hon?" he said as they stood across from each other reaching up for apples. He leaned over to retrieve a leaf caught in her hair.

Laura smiled. It was the full-of-sweetness smile McCabe

hadn't seen for a while. "Yes, it is. I'm so happy you were able to take some time off to get this done. I was a little worried the apples were going to rot before we had a chance to get to them."

"You could say I made a few demands. I told Sheriff Medrano if I didn't have some time off, he was going to be working with a very unhappy man." McCabe chuckled, but he was serious. He loved his wife and was willing to do anything necessary to keep her happy.

"That would make two of us. I was beginning to feel neglected. I know it's silly, Tim, but since you retired I was used to spending extra time with you, and I've hated giving that up. It's been pretty lonely. There's just so many hours I can fill volunteering at the museum."

"Maybe I made a mistake, Laura. For gosh sakes, you know I would never let a job come between us. You're the most important person in my life. Seems like maybe that's what has been happening lately. I was so caught up in being back in law enforcement that I wasn't even considering how you might be feeling about it."

"Well, now you know. I surely wouldn't want you to give up something that you love to do, Tim. Maybe you could just take on half of what's offered and let someone else do the rest."

He reached over to touch her hand. "Done. Don't want my best girl playing second fiddle to anyone." McCabe retrieved two buckets filled with apples and climbed down the ladder. Before he could dump them into the waiting crates, the housekeeper waved from the porch.

"Señor McCabe, there's some people at the gate to see you, and they say it's important. Should I let them in?" she said.

"That's all right, Anna. Tell them I'll be just a minute." He caught Laura's exasperated glance. "I'm sure it's nothing, Dear. Let me take care of it and I'll be right back."

McCabe figured the visitors weren't from the Sheriff's office, as they normally called on his cell phone when they needed him. Probably someone from the gallery. It wasn't unusual for the manager to send clients to their home to discuss a particular object they might be interested in purchasing. Whoever it was, he was determined to deal with them quickly and get back to spending time with his wife.

McCabe thumbed the code into the pad next to the kitchen door to open the gates and allow the unannounced visitors onto the main driveway. A dark van, an SUV and a black sedan rolled slowly down the circular driveway toward him. The windows were tinted and he couldn't make out any of the occupants. Before he had a chance to step down from the porch to greet them, the doors of the SUV opened and four men armed with automatic weapons jumped out into the drive.

"Tim McCabe, hold it right there," one of the men shouted, brandishing his weapon.

"Whoa, there," said McCabe. "What's going on here?" He put his arms up in mock surrender but quickly realized the seriousness of the situation.

The back doors of the dark sedan opened and a woman and two men dressed in dark suits walked up to him. They flashed FBI badges. "Don't move, Mr. McCabe. Stay right where you are," the stocky agent hollered.

"Am I in some kind of trouble, gentlemen? I believe I paid IRS what I owed them," he said.

"Tim McCabe, we have a warrant for your arrest for transporting and selling archaeological artifacts. In addition, we're here to serve you with a copy of the search warrant issued by the Federal Grand Jury for this residence and the gallery located at nine eleven Canyon Road." Agent John Reddy read McCabe his rights while the other handcuffed him.

Laura McCabe ran to her husband. "Oh my God, Tim. What's happening here?"

"Laura, go inside and call Baker Snead. Tell him to get over here fast. I'll explain to you as soon as I figure it out myself," McCabe said.

The agent blocked Laura's path. "Excuse me, Ma'am. Nobody enters the house until the search and seizure has been completed. Please do not touch anything," the female agent said to Laura.

"That's all right, Laura, use the phone in the Hummer," said McCabe. "I don't know what this is about, but we'll get to the bottom of it."

The agents unloaded boxes, plastic bags and bins from the van and wheeled them toward the door. McCabe stood outside in the yard, feeling completely helpless as they stormed through the house dislodging the cat and the housekeeper in their wake. He saw the futility of saying anything further. *Just what the hell were they looking for?*

Chapter Twenty-Four

The UNM Lobos were ahead of the NMSU Aggies by three points. Without a score by the Aggies in the final minutes, there was little hope they would add another notch to their winning streak. Lieutenant Romero let out a whoop, took a swig of his Corona and then raised the bottle toward the radio in a toast to his alma mater as the final buzzer sounded. His Lobos had won again.

Romero was ecstatic as he prepared dinner, dicing white onions to sauté with the pound of liver purchased earlier at Albertson's. When the house phone rang, he debated whether to answer it. Probably someone wanting to sell him tickets to the Shrine Circus or begging money for one cause or another. It was that time of year. Telemarketers always seemed to know the minute he arrived home. With the basketball game over, he switched the station on the mini-boombox in the corner to a country western song. Some Johnny-Come-Lately was singing about his hard luck in the morning sun. He lowered the volume and then reached for the phone, intending to cut them off at the pass.

"Hello," he said.

"Thank God I found you," said the shaky voice on the other end of the line.

"Laura, is that you? What's wrong?"

"The FBI just arrested Tim, or took him downtown for questioning, I don't know," she could barely get the words out.

Romero was incredulous. "What? Are you sure?"

"I was right there, Rick. They came to the house." Laura began to weep softly. "I'm sorry. It was just so awful. We were picking apples. Just spending some time together, talking about everything and nothing. And then they drove up in a bunch of black cars. They looked so ominous. I didn't hear everything they said. They wouldn't even let me go into the house to use the phone to call our attorney."

"Are you all right, Laura? Is there someone there with you?" Romero said.

"Yes, yes. I'm in the house now. I'm all right. I can't believe it. Tim being taken away as though he was a common criminal." She stifled a sob.

"Listen to me, Laura. Where is Tim now?"

"They took him. Put him in a black SUV and took him. The others stayed in the house, wrapping up all the pots and things, putting them in boxes and loading them into the van. They stripped the house of everything we've ever collected. They even took the old Santo, which has sat on the table in the hallway since we moved here. I haven't the faintest idea what they were looking for, but they took it all. Every single piece." Her voice cracked.

"Are you sure it was the FBI?"

"Yes, Yes. The FBI. That's how the woman identified herself."

"The agent was a woman?"

"Yes, one of them. I have her card. Just a minute. I put it on the counter."

Romero waited patiently while Laura walked to the kitchen. She picked up the extension phone. "Here it is. FBI Special Agent Sandra Gorman. G-O-R-M-A-N."

Romero was livid. He cursed under his breath. *Son of a bitch.* "Thank you, Laura. Now you try to get some rest. Everything's going to be all right. I'll get back to you as soon as I know something." Romero hung up the phone.

"Dammit," he said, flipping through the day timer on his desk. He found Sandra's card and punched the numbers on his cell phone. It rang for such a long time he expected it to go to message. He was caught off guard when he heard a male voice on the other end.

"This is Lieutenant Romero, Santa Fe County Sheriff's Office, may I speak to Agent Gorman?" he said.

"Hey, Rick. How's it hanging, Brother." It was Carlos.

"Not in the mood, Carlos. Let me talk to Agent Gorman."

"She's indisposed at the moment. I can have her call you in the morning."

"Carlos, put her on the damn phone or I'll be pounding on her door in the next ten minutes." Romero had reached the end of his patience, and as usual Carlos had a way of pushing his buttons. All fun and games. Nothing serious about this guy. Two years in jail hadn't taught him much.

"All right, man. Keep your shirt on," Carlos said.

ೞ

"Who the hell is it, Carlos?" Sandra wrapped the towel around her dripping torso, a fetching sight for Carlos' eyes.

"My brother, the Lieutenant. He sounds a little agitated, like someone gave him a wedgie." Carlos handed her the phone.

"Well, hello, Detective Romero," she cooed into the phone. "What can I assist you with?"

"You know damned well what I'm calling about, Agent Gorman. Your people arrested my partner, Tim McCabe."

"Call me Sandra, after all, We're almost family," she winked at Carlos, who was entertaining himself by planting a slow trail of kisses, beginning at her toes and working his way up.

Romero sounded even more annoyed. "I'd like to see you in my office in the morning."

"Sure thing, I'll be there around ten," she said. "I plan on sleeping in, if you know what I mean."

"Nine o'clock," Romero said. The call ended abruptly.

"What does my dear brother have his shorts all in a twist about, Sandra?" Carlos said.

She caressed his cheek to reassure him that the call hadn't ruined the moment. "Nothing to worry your sweet little head about, Carlos. Official business. Seems we arrested a friend of his. I'll work it out in the morning," she said. "Now, get that enticing booty of yours over here."

At two minutes to nine the next morning Sandra Gorman screeched into the parking lot of the satellite office. She had only slept for a few hours and would have preferred to stay in bed snuggled up to Carlos. Maybe she'd go back to the hotel after her meeting. She wasn't punching a time card, anyway. She checked her makeup in the visor mirror, reapplied a fresh coat of lipstick, licked her lips, and headed for the door.

Lieutenant Romero was waiting for her in his office. "Come in, Agent Gorman. Have a seat," he said.

She waited for an offer of coffee. When it wasn't forthcoming, she helped herself, deliberately taking her sweet time to stir in the cream and sugar.

"Have a seat," Romero repeated. It was obvious he was still irritated about her participation in the previous day's events. He was having a difficult time remaining focused. If she had been a man, she thought, he would have decked her. "All right, Gorman. What can you tell me about Tim McCabe's arrest?"

"Nothing, really. FBI business," she said, looking straight at him and taking a slow sip of her coffee.

"Come on, you mean to say you can't tell me what's going on here? That's a crock and you know it. The least you could have done was give me a heads up. We could have arranged for McCabe to meet you with his attorneys."

"You know I couldn't do that. He might have disposed of any evidence we would have collected from his house."

"You're referring to a fellow police officer here, an upstanding citizen, not some street scum," Romero said. "Even when he sat across from you at our last meeting, you knew all about what was going to happen. There was no need to show up at his house all gung ho and scare the crap out of everyone."

"I'll admit that at the time of our meeting things were in the early stages of development, yes. Look, Detective Romero, my hands were tied. I was just following orders. I wasn't about to put my job on the line by revealing an impending search warrant, associate or not."

"I'm sure it's a double-edged sword. McCabe's the last person anyone should suspect of any wrongdoing," he said.

"Hey, life's full of little surprises, Detective," she said. "He might appear to be Mister Clean on the surface, but our investigation revealed he could very well be involved in some shady transactions, along with a whole slew of other dealers in that field. We didn't just pull this shit out of a hat."

"I understand that this is the culmination of a long and somewhat tedious investigation. I didn't just fall off the chili express, Agent Gorman. I am familiar with how investigations are conducted. But there are extenuating circumstances that might preclude a particular person from being considered a suspect, and McCabe fits in that category."

"That's bullshit and you know it. We can't pick and choose who we consider a suspect. Bottom line, the wheels are already in motion, and there's not a hell of a lot I can do about it at this point," she retorted.

"You could have handled it differently," Romero shot back.

"You have a lot of nerve singling me out for your little rant. I wasn't the only agent involved."

"Look, I'm sure I need to apologize for jumping all over you. This hit a little too close to home. But I do appreciate your coming by this morning, Agent Gorman. I'll just have to approach it from another direction." Romero rolled his chair back and tossed his cup in the trash.

Sandra stood up. "That's it? You drag me all the way over here to rake me through the coals? You not only question my authority but my abilities, and then you treat me like some sort of rookie and dismiss me? For your information, Lieutenant Detective Romero, as a Special Agent with the FBI, I have conducted a number of Federal criminal investigations. We've been on this case for over five years. McCabe is part of the fallout. I'm sorry it had to happen to him, but he's in the business of collecting and selling prehistoric artifacts which are protected under Federal law. We don't have a Good Boy pass for people some detectives might think are above the law."

"All right, all right. I get the picture. Let's call a truce here. Again, I apologize for anything I said to upset you."

"And another thing, Lieutenant Romero," Sandra continued. "You can bet your brown ass that as soon as I've filed my reports for the cases we've been consulting on, I'll be glad to kiss this hick town adios."

CR

Romero inhaled deeply and let out a long whistle as he heard the door slam behind her. He'd been tempted to comment about the ramifications of putting her job on the line by dating a felon, but had held his tongue, knowing it wouldn't have helped his argument.

"Women," he said. "No, make that Women FBI Agents."

Chapter Twenty-Five

The headlines on the front page of the morning newspaper all but accused Santa Fe dealer and gallery owner Tim McCabe of archaeological looting. The FBI and special agents from the National Park Service had searched the homes of several Santa Fe residents, including McCabe. The article went on to say that agents seized not only his personal computers and business records, but over fifty boxes of Native American artifacts collected by McCabe and his wife, Laura.

Of the many dealers and collectors singled out by the FBI for random searches, McCabe was the last person even his peers would have suspected of wrongdoing. He was the straightest of the straight shooters, and the single most authority on all matters prehistoric. A tremor measuring 5.0 on the Richter scale reverberated through the tribal arts community. If the FBI would investigate someone as upstanding as Tim McCabe, who else could they have in their sights? It was no secret that any time a dealer or collector was involved in publicity regarding allegations of wrongdoing—no matter how insignificant or ill perceived—the mere innuendo served to corrupt their credibility. More damaging though would be the effect the accusations would have on the upcoming ethnographic shows, which featured hundreds of dealers throughout the United States hawking their finds, much of the material exactly what the Feds were currently examining under their microscopes. Disreputable dealers would just crawl back under their rocks until things cooled down.

Romero was aware that the U.S. District Attorney had unearthed a number of unproven allegations about McCabe, all fairly circumstantial. But in Santa Fe County, all you had to do was repeat something twice before it took on the aura of truth. He tossed the newspaper in the waste basket.

He called out to his assistant. "Clarissa! Get Dave Chavez on the phone, would you?"

Clarissa stuck her head in the door. "Sheesh, boss, you're scaring all the birds away hollering like that."

"Very funny. Just get Dave on the phone for me, please," he repeated.

"Lighten up. The pizza guy or the DA?"

"Enough. The USDA, and if you say where's the beef, I'm going to fire your ass."

Five minutes later, Clarissa buzzed him. "Dave Chavez on the line," she said sweetly.

"Hey Dave, Detective Rick Romero, Santa Fe County Sheriff's Office," he said, reaching for his cigarettes. Clarissa pushed open the windows and turned on the fan. Romero ignored her and motioned for her to get out.

"Long time no speak, Amigo. I see you're still hanging around the Sheriff's Office. Bucking for the Sheriff's job, are we?" Chavez said.

Romero chuckled. "You know Sheriff Medrano's in for the duration. I'm just the hired help. You still on the Federal dole?"

"Yeah, leave it to the Feds. Nobody moves up the ladder unless somebody retires or dies. So, Rick, is this a social call or you digging for info?" Chavez snickered.

"Digging."

"Shoot. I'm all ears."

"I'm calling about my partner, Tim McCabe. I understand you're working the antiquities case here in Santa Fe."

"Yeah, that's one of my recently acquired case files. I've only had a chance to skim through it. I wasn't aware he was in law enforcement."

"He's a retired veteran police officer from Idaho. Been in New Mexico for some time. Longtime friend of Sheriff Medrano, and a good man to boot. He signed on with us a while back as a special investigator. Sheriff Medrano will tell you we're lucky to have him. Not only that, he's a hundred percent honest in every facet of his life."

"Ninety percent of the individuals we arrest claim to be good men."

Romero shifted in his chair. "This one is. Look, Dave, according to the warrant, you seized everything from pots to pendants in McCabe's house. I would bet you a year's salary that everything was purchased legitimately."

"Yes, and everything on that list is illegal. I assure you we've got enough to issue an indictment."

"You are aware that McCabe owns about two hundred acres adjacent to the old Crawford Ranch in Cerrillos, sixty of which comprise San Lazaro Pueblo Indian ruins? It's the only privately owned prehistoric ruin in the area."

"Yeah, I'm aware of that. So?"

"I'm no attorney, but I'm pretty sure I heard somewhere it wasn't illegal to remove artifacts from your own property, especially if you didn't sell them."

"Let me interject something here, Rick. The Feds have been building their case for the past five years. They've been focusing primarily on looters from the Four-Corners area who make it their pastime to dig up graves and pillage sites on public lands. That included a number of the ancient pueblos in Northern New Mexico. Pretty much all of what they dig up illegally is sold to dealers and collectors, whether privately or at one of the regional ethno shows, McCabe included. All of this goes against the provisions of the Federal Antiquities Act."

"Crissake, Dave. It's common knowledge around the entire southwest that McCabe is on a different level than the run-of-the-mill looters you're talking about. He's been working hand in hand with the University on the digs at San Lazaro and every single item their crew has dug up has been photographed and documented. McCabe published a comprehensive book last year chronicling his finds from the very beginning." Romero was so worked up he almost choked on the next swallow of coffee.

"I'm not disputing that, Rick. McCabe just happens to be part of the aftershock. We can't give special treatment to anyone, especially if it's going to put our case in jeopardy."

Romero felt as though he was spinning on black ice. Friend or no friend, it didn't seem that his old childhood pal was going to be very forthcoming. "So what can you assure me of, Dave? Is this thing going to go the full nine yards? Is he going to have to lawyer up and spend tens of thousands of dollars fighting something that won't amount to a hill of beans in the end?"

"Hard to say. We don't have everything back from our agents yet. They still have another residence to inspect, but the guy's sitting on the beach somewhere in Rio."

"I know you can't divulge your informant's name, but I just happen to know that of the six people whose homes were searched in Santa Fe, the informant's house was one of them. That's a pretty good cover up in itself. It wouldn't go very well for the Feds' case if this guy's name accidentally slipped to the media, particularly when everyone in that circle knows who he is."

"That would be dirty pool, Rick. Something I wouldn't expect from you."

"Hey, Dave, I'm just grasping at straws here. I'm not his attorney. Just his friend. And you and I are friends. As far as I'm concerned, this conversation is off the record. I'm just telling you that they could very well decide to play the media card if it would serve to divert attention from McCabe. That's what happens when you use an informant whose credibility leaves a lot to be desired. I can't tell you how many times the Department's been burned in those same circumstances."

"I'll tell you what. Between you, me and the wall, I'm not planning on pursuing McCabe's involvement in anything other than his purchase of a sacred object from a known archaeological site. If he will agree to return the first item on the list, the Zuni ceremonial fetish, my office will work toward having it repatriated to the tribe. He'll have to eat the money he shelled out for it," Chavez said.

"That sounds more than fair to me," Romero said, about to break into a jig.

"Have his attorney get in touch with my office and we'll work out the details and make arrangements for the confiscated material to be returned before it ends up at a warehouse in Hoboken. Good enough?"

Romero breathed a sigh of relief. "Good enough. I owe you one."

"You owe me two. It's double-stamp day," Chavez chuckled.

Romero smiled at the reference to their short-lived teenaged careers as sack boys for the last of the Piggly-Wiggly grocery stores in New Mexico.

"You got it," he said.

Romero hung up the phone and wiped his forehead. He noticed how tight the muscles in his neck were. The throbbing pain in his shoulder didn't help much, either. "Clarissa," he hollered. "Get Tim McCabe on the phone for me, please."

Clarissa smacked her forehead with the palm of her hand. "Sheesh, you're in rare form today, Boss. Guess we might as well yank out that expensive intercom system you had the phone company install. Maybe two empty cans and a string would work just as well."

"Just make the call, Clarissa. I still don't know which button to push to get an outside line," Romero said, a sheepish grin on his face.

"It's the one marked 'outside line,' Rick," she smirked. "Tim McCabe's on line one."

"How you doing there, Tim? You sound a little jagged around the edges."

"Just a little frustrated. It's taking me awhile to absorb this FBI thing. I don't know who's worse, them or the IRS. Both agencies have a knack for aging a person ten years," he said, forcing a laugh.

"Well, I might just have some good news for you on that front."

"I could use some good news, Amigo. Let her rip," McCabe said.

"I can't go into too much detail, but I just got off the phone with the Feds. Good friend of mine happens to be in charge of this investigation. We had a long conversation, and to give you the shorthand version, they're willing to dismiss the case against you if you'll agree to return the ceremonial fetish to the Zunis."

"I'd be willing to return the whole darned collection just to get them off my butt," McCabe said, the hint of resignation in his voice moving up the scale.

"Well, you won't have to go that far. Just that one piece. Tell your attorney to contact Head Agent David Chavez. Clarissa can get you his number."

McCabe was overcome with relief. "I don't know how I can thank you for going to bat for me with the Feds, Rick. I wasn't sure just where this drama was going to end. I had flashbacks of joining some of our criminal compadres at the Federal Detention Center in Albuquerque."

"Hey, just glad I could be of help. None of this should have happened. I'm sorry you had to go through it."

"It wasn't so much me. It freaked Laura out pretty good."

"She doing all right?"

"She'll be okay once I give her the good news. And if she has her way, we won't be purchasing any more material, historic or otherwise, for a long while," he laughed, this time with gusto.

"Probably not a bad idea," Romero said. He was grateful he'd been able to repay McCabe for his past kindnesses, although he hadn't thought it would involve keeping him out of jail.

Chapter Twenty-Six

With the air conditioner blowing full force, Carlos leaned back in the easy chair in Sandra's downtown hotel suite. Rivulets of sweat poured down his bare chest. The ashtray on the table next to him overflowed with cigarette butts. There seemed to be little he could do to dissuade Sandra from leaving Santa Fe and returning to San Francisco.

"Hey, Babe. I thought we were hitting it off," he said, gently stroking her arm. "That's quite a bombshell you just dropped in my lap."

Sandra wasn't meeting his gaze. "Look, Carlos. Don't take this personal. We both knew it wasn't going to last."

"You're saying it was just a fling? I ended almost two years of forced celibacy only to be dumped by the first woman I date? That's pretty hilarious." Carlos grunted.

"To be completely honest, the only place we were hitting it off was in the sack. Do you realize we've spent more time having sex than we have anything else? With the exception of our first date at the Airport, we've never gone out to dinner again," Sandra said, pacing the floor as she spoke. She was avoiding his eyes and choosing her words with care. Carlos suspected she was afraid of him. After all, with his "criminal" past, he'd have a low boiling point, right?

Carlos flashed a half-smile at her. "I thought we were both enjoying ourselves. I know for sure you were feeling it."

"That's not the point, Carlos. It would be nice to interact with the rest of the world once in a while. For the past month

I've gone from the office to the hotel, nowhere else, not even a movie."

"Hey, wait a minute, Sandra. That's a little harsh. I may not be one of those sensitive types you're used to, but I can see you're putting the blame on me for something I'm not guilty of. Correct me if I'm wrong, but I asked you a bunch of times what you wanted to do and we always ended up in bed and then ordering room service." Carlos' mind was racing, trying to figure out what brought on this sudden change of heart. "I've made a few plans of late, and they all included you to some degree or another."

"You're right. I'm sorry. This isn't about you." Sandra sat down on the edge of the bed.

"What is it about, then, Sandra? My brother have something to do with this? Has he been giving you a hard time?" It would be just like Rick to throw a monkey wrench in his first relationship. His dislike for Sandra was pretty obvious.

"Look, Carlos. It's nothing like that. Your brother has absolutely nothing to do with my decision. I realized I'm not happy working in Santa Fe. Other than you, there's not enough of a challenge here. I miss the bright lights and the social life. I'm bored with the routine here in the Land of Mañana. Even law enforcement moves at a snail's pace. They take their sweet time investigating cases and don't give a damn whether they're solved or not."

Carlos walked across the room and out to the veranda overlooking the swimming pool. The afternoon heat was stifling. He lit a cigarette and exhaled a long puff of smoke, which curled into ringlets and hung in the air until the breeze escorted it out across the yard. When he went back into the room, he shivered. It felt like a freezer. He studied her quizzically. "Can we talk about this? I'm open to making a move if it will help things along."

"There's nothing you can say that will change my mind,

Carlos. I'm not willing to ask you to move away from here. It wouldn't work out. I've given it a lot of thought."

"A lot of thought? You mean from last night to this morning? Yesterday you were all torqued about running off to Acapulco for the weekend. I called my probation officer and he said it would be okay." He snuffed out the cigarette and lit another. "I was just about to pick the tickets up at the travel service."

"Things are different. Today is another day. A lot has happened," she sighed.

Carlos held back the torrent of anger ready to spew from his mouth. "Did you get a midnight visit from someone I should know about, or should I say *someone* I don't know about? It seems like everything between us changed in just the few hours you were out of my sight." He tried to appear nonchalant, but his voice was weighted with despair. He couldn't let her know he was jealous.

⊂⊃

Sandra shrugged her shoulders, reached for a bottle of water, and swallowed a double dose of aspirin. The more she continued to talk, the more her head pounded. She decided she might as well be truthful with Carlos, but she still wasn't sure what his reaction was going to be. Instead she merely said, "I've cleared all the files I was assigned here. Nothing more for me to do. I'm being reassigned to California. I leave tomorrow morning."

The truth be told, Robert Jackson, Sandra's San Francisco flame, had called the night before. The conversation went straight from hello into how much he missed her and was ready to commit to their relationship. He had a lot more to offer than Carlos did, and hey, first and foremost, she was a material girl. Carlos was all right, but he wasn't the type of guy she could ever bring home to Daddy. He was a fling. *Period.*

"Well, there you have it," Carlos said. "Was that so hard? I'm open to chocking up some frequent flyer miles in the next few months, Sweetheart. Would you consider me doing that? I could come up on weekends at first and then if things work out, I could make a permanent move."

"Listen to yourself, Carlos. First of all you have to check in with a probation officer every month. Secondly, you don't have a job and from where I sit, you haven't been looking for one, either. You live with your brother. You don't have any visible means of support and any future prospects."

Sandra felt like shouting, but she kept her voice calm. *Christ.* That would be the last thing she wanted—to have a guy attach himself to her rising star, a guy just released from prison at that.

This is my boyfriend, Carlos. He's a felon, but isn't he handsome?

Carlos was visibly pissed. "Well, excuse me all to hell. I didn't know we were keeping score. Maybe we should just leave it at that. You do whatever you need to do, Sandra. Chase after that rainbow, find the pot of gold. Who gives a blue shit. I'm out of here. Thanks for the ride."

Sandra didn't see the need to respond. She had accomplished what she set out to do. Carlos slammed the door on his way out.

Such a shame. Didn't even kiss her goodbye.

She picked up the phone and dialed the airline.

Chapter Twenty-Seven

Nine years earlier, on June 21, 2001, just after noon, Jeff Whitney had flicked the light switch as he stepped into the master bedroom of the Ilfeld home. Like Rose's garden, it was as neat as a pin. Not a thing was out of place. The digital clock and a small lamp on the side table remained undisturbed. Fuzzy pink slippers peeked out from the edge of the chenille bedspread. You could tell Rose was an immaculate housekeeper by the way the chrome fixtures in the master bathroom gleamed. The living room, however, was a different story. Everything was in disarray. Don Ilfeld sat slumped on the couch next to his wife's lifeless body, his head resting heavily on his hands.

"You have to help me, Jeff. It was an accident. I swear I didn't mean to kill her. She just wouldn't shut up. She knew about Kitty and was threatening to divorce me. I kept telling her I would end it, and we could patch up our marriage. Things got out of control. She was like a crazy woman, pushing and scratching at me. I lost it. I started choking her and couldn't stop." Ilfeld's demeanor was a mere shred of the machismo he generally displayed. He was sweating profusely and his hands were shaking.

Whitney was disgusted. He thought about leaving Ilfeld to take the fall for this, then he thought about what Don knew about him. Tit for tat. Helping his cowardly friend was the price, then.

"Shut up for a minute, Don. Let me think. This stinks.

No way is anyone going to believe choking someone to death is an accident. A scandal like this is going to cost you your job and the promotion coming up next month—maybe your freedom for the rest of your life. On the other hand, you could make all those lies you've been telling about how sick she's been work in your favor."

Whitney paced across the floor. He looked toward the street though the French doors and then at the body.

"It didn't start out that way. Everyone kept asking why she wasn't attending any of the events. I ran out of excuses. Couldn't tell them she was pissed at me for stepping out on her and that she was thinking of divorce, could I?" Ilfeld looked up at Whitney, his eyes puffy and red.

"If you'd kept it in your pants you wouldn't be in this mess. You know how the Department feels about screwing around with the hired help."

"I know, I know. But—"

"Cut the bullshit, Ilfeld. You're acting like a damned crybaby."

Don looked up at Whitney. He could see what he was thinking: *I've kept my mouth shut all this time.*

"Now listen up. The best I can come up with right now is that we put Rose in the car. You drive down the highway toward town and take the first exit. See if you can ram into that big cottonwood tree in the field next to the fence without killing yourself. I'll drive up behind you and report it as an accident. By the time the ambulance arrives, she'll be lying on the ground, dead."

Ilfeld looked up at him. "You think it will work, Whit?"

Whitney threw his hands up in exasperation. "What else you got, genius? You'd better get your ass in gear. She's starting to stiffen up. Take a look outside and make sure none of the neighbors are working in their yards. That hedge next to the driveway should give us enough cover."

"I don't know how to thank you for helping me out of

this jam, Whit." Ilfeld held his hand out to Whitney.

As if I had a choice.

"Don't be thanking me yet. Both our asses might be in a sling if we don't pull this off. Now hurry up and get the hell out of here."

Chapter Twenty-Eight

Although Jerry Frazier was dead, Jemimah felt compelled to fill in the blanks of his life. She drove down Alameda Street, into the driveway of a small subdivision packed with one-story tract houses. As she looked around, she spotted a man trimming trees in his front yard. She walked over and introduced herself.

"You a cop?" the man asked.

"No, I'm just an investigator, looking for information on your neighbor, Jerry Frazier."

He gave her a strange look. "You mean the guy they found dead in a field?"

"Yes, that's the one. Your neighbor. Can I ask you a few questions? I won't take much of your time."

"Sure, I guess. I got nothing to hide."

"What did you think of Mr. Frazier?"

"Well, you know, he was kind of an odd bird."

"In what way?"

"Pretty much kept to himself. Didn't say hello unless you said it first," he said. "And even then he would just grunt."

"I understand he worked as a gardener or in some similar profession, landscaping, maybe?"

"Yeah, you couldn't tell it by looking at his own yard, though. Almost every morning he loaded his tools into that old yellow truck and drove off. Wouldn't come back until after dark. Then one day he up and moved out of town and didn't come back for a long time. Place was rented out pretty much the whole time he was gone. Frazier moved back into his house a couple of years ago and then got sick or something."

"Did he have a family?"

"Not that I know of. As I said, he pretty much kept to himself. I can't say we ever had a conversation that consisted of more than ten words."

"Any recent visitors?"

"Nope, never saw anyone drive up, hardly ever. Just the guy who brought him food every day, and he would just leave the tray on that table near the door," he said. "I don't think they saw much of him, either. He was just a name on their delivery list."

"Anyone else?"

"Oh, there was this Indian guy who used to come by on a motorcycle every once in a while."

"Indian as in Native American?"

"Yeah, you know, like cowboys and Indians. Stocky guy. He had a long braid and all. Drove a big ass Harley. You could hear him coming down the street for a mile."

"Seen him lately?"

"No, not for quite a while. They used to sit on the porch and drink beer and smoke. Could smell that damned smoke all the way into my living room." He picked up a shovel full of manure. "Smelled a lot like pot, but I was never sure so I didn't make a big deal of it."

"How long ago was that?"

"Oh, I don't know. Guess it was before he got sick. Seems like after that, nobody ever came to see him. House and yard went to hell, too." He bent his head down and returned to his yard work, a silent cue that he was done talking to Jemimah.

"Just one more question," she said. "Can you think of anyone who might want to hurt Mr. Frazier?"

"The guy probably pissed a few people off with his arrogant attitude, but I don't think any of his visitors would have hurt him," he said. "I never heard any arguments coming from his direction."

"Thank you. You've been a great help." Jemimah put the notebook in her jacket pocket.

A few days before, Detective Romero had informed her that the crime scene was virtually useless. If there had been anything worth recovering, the rain washed it down into the arroyo. *Maybe this was just a random crime*, she thought.

Coincidental, but random nonetheless. She still couldn't conceive of someone killing Frazier, but she agreed with Detective Romero that he might have been killed somewhere else. That was probably something they would never know, thanks to Mother Nature's unwelcome diligence in covering up the killer's tracks.

Chapter Twenty-Nine

A news item on Jerry Frazier's murder was relegated to a two inch column on the last page of the local newspaper. An article about an upcoming art event filled two pages. Even less noticeable was the two-line obituary:

Jerry Frazier, 62, died Tuesday. Services pending.

All that was left to indicate that he had once been a resident on earth was a toe tag as he was tucked into a cold metal drawer in the basement of the County Morgue.

Frazier's service was as low key as one could be. Only a few seats in the chapel of the funeral home were occupied. The funeral director, his wife, Detective Romero and Jemimah were present, along with the fellow on the motorcycle the neighbor had mentioned. The eulogy was short, and the scriptures chosen appropriate for a man who had been ill for the last years of his life and then cruelly murdered.

Acting as substitute for a pastor, the funeral director assured those in attendance that Jerry Frazier was now in a better place.

Jemimah wasn't so sure. She continued to wonder if she had been successful in contacting him sooner, he might still be alive. She kicked herself for initially believing that Frazier had an underlying motive for coming to see her. Nonetheless, she felt compelled to foot the bill. He deserved more than a simple wooden casket provided by the County. The generic service lasted for less than thirty minutes. Nobody knew Frazier's religious preference or even if he had one. At the conclusion of the service, the funeral director popped in a CD of "Amazing Grace."

Frazier was to be buried in the pauper's cemetery on the southwest side of Santa Fe, a desolate plot of land where unmarked graves outnumbered those with faded inscriptions on cardboard or simple wooden crosses. Its graves were rarely visited. Every couple of years, members of a local Boy Scouts' troop would come and remove the weeds, fulfilling the requirements for a civic duty patch.

As they walked toward the car, Jemimah said, "I feel sorry about Frazier. You would have thought he'd touched more people in his lifetime."

"I agree," Romero said. "You'd think some of his neighbors would have stopped by to see him off, or maybe the people he worked for."

"Maybe he had nothing to do with them. Hard to say. Anyway, it's a moot subject now," Jemimah said.

Chapter Thirty

In the days following his date with Chief Suazo's voluptuous secretary, Captain Jeff Whitney avoided State Police Headquarters and had yet to answer any of Patsy's calls. He had bigger fish to fry and was in the middle of devising his plan.

As he drove toward the east end of Santa Fe, he was cool and collected. Whitney had thought he knew Ilfeld like the back of his hand, but then Ilfeld had screwed everything up by changing his story when Jemimah interviewed him. All she had to do was flash that pretty smile of hers and he'd melt into a puddle and tell her more than everything she wanted to know, at the same time hoping he had a chance of getting laid.

Whitney also knew everything about Jemimah. He'd been keeping track of every move she'd made for a couple of weeks now. He knew everyone she spoke to and who she interviewed. He was beginning to think he had underestimated her in every respect. He was both impressed and annoyed by the progress she seemed to be making on the case.

The problem was, Jemimah wasn't sharing information with anyone on the force. Not even Detective Romero. Whitney wished he'd understood that before he'd gone to so much trouble to use the guy for target practice. Jemimah seemed to avoid him at all costs. The less Romero knew, the better. It was likely she was reserving the glory of solving the case for herself. Whitney couldn't let her do that. There was too much at stake.

Whitney was a no-nonsense cop. Once he said something, he never backed down. *Look them straight in the eye, tell your story and stick to it.* He knew that no matter how this thing played out, Ilfeld was up to his ass in circumstantial evidence. No witnesses. No conclusive autopsy.

Problem was, if Ilfeld cracked, he would take Whitney down with him. Should have let that SOB face the music instead of getting involved by trying to help him. He'd probably be out of jail by now on an involuntary manslaughter charge.

Not that he'd had a choice.

He turned right at the last traffic light on St. Francis drive and headed east past the old cemetery. Out of the corner of his eye he could see multi-colored pinwheels spinning on some of the graves as the wind revved up. Whitney didn't care for cemeteries. He'd stood at attention at too many funerals for too many police officers for too many years.

He drove out beyond the city onto Hyde Park Road toward the Ski Basin. The shadows of the Sangre de Cristo Mountains on the narrow road made an otherwise sunny day appear cloudy and overcast. The cool mountain air was exactly what Whitney needed to clear his head. He paid little attention to hikers who walked on the path near where he was parked probably wondering what a State Police vehicle was doing parked up in the hills. He let them wonder, didn't even acknowledge their waved greetings. Maybe they were thinking some poor hiker was lost, or somebody had been murdered nearby. Hell, maybe they thought he was sitting in his car, jacking off. Who the hell cared?

As the sun made serious overtures toward setting, Whitney drove back down the ever winding ski basin road and headed to the north end of the 599 bypass. It took another hour to retrieve his shiny maroon Lexus from the parking garage at police headquarters and then head home. He was off duty for the weekend. He wound his way up Don Gaspar Avenue to Palace Avenue and the rear entrance of a two-story Santa Fe style condo nestled between two bed and breakfasts. The condo suited his purposes. He'd signed a lease and paid a year in advance. Even when he did take women there, he drove around in circles a few times, distracting them with caresses and conversation so they couldn't find the place on their own. A little paranoid, perhaps, but there were few things that annoyed Whitney more than women who expected a phone call or a second date. If they met his initial requirements, he saw them again. If they failed to meet his standards, he didn't. Few ever returned.

Situated in a valley surrounded by high mountain ranges, the city of Santa Fe doesn't have many tall buildings around its central plaza and for that matter, even in surrounding neighborhoods. Some antiquated ordinance or another precluded edifices of a certain height in the historic downtown area, so the ways of committing suicide by jumping off a tall building or pushing someone out of a seventh story window to make it appear like a suicide were limited. But there were other ways to end a life, and Whitney was thinking seriously about that.

He trudged up two flights of steps to a long portal with a wrought iron railing placed between faux adobe pillars. Number seven was the last unit at the end. Whitney unlocked the dead bolt and stepped into the dimly lit living room. It was sparsely furnished with a leather couch, a chair and a recliner. The place smelled of old take-out and stale cigarette smoke. He cranked the windows open and looked out onto the flagstone patio below. It made little difference to him that the yard was profuse with multi-colored rose bushes. A stocky teenager waved to a woman on the balcony above as he hollered out, "Don't wait up for me, Mom." Whitney stared at him.

"Don't wait up for me, Jeff." That was the last thing his mother had ever said to him. Oh, she had used the expression before, but that was the last time. It had been their private joke, one they even called out when they went to the bathroom. For as long as he could remember, his mother worked late hours waiting tables at one of the local greasy spoons. Most days, as he arrived home from school, she would just be leaving for work. As she walked out the door, she would reach over and give her son a fond embrace and make him promise to do his homework, be sure all the doors were locked and get to bed early.

When she didn't come home that night, he stayed by the window and waited. He sat there for two days until he saw a black and white police car drive up and park in front of the house. He never saw her again. Not even at the funeral home. It was a closed casket. Her body was mangled beyond recognition. All that remained was a photograph of the two of them taken on his eighth birthday the previous year.

There were no witnesses to the assault on his mother in the parking lot of the restaurant. She had been beaten mercilessly and left to die for no more than her meager share of the tip jar, which had been split between the employees on that shift. Her car was found ten miles away in a ravine on a deserted patch of land. The murder went unsolved for eight years, until a transient arrested for kidnapping and murdering a woman in the same vicinity confessed to killing Jeff Whitney's mother.

The young orphan Whit spent the next ten years of his life with his uncle's family on a ranch in El Paso. After a four year stint in the military, Whitney entered the Dallas DPS Academy and eventually moved to New Mexico. He was now a twenty year veteran of the State Police, and at the moment, prospects of his eventual retirement were looking a little shaky.

He laid the 9mm Glock on the table in the living room

and walked into the kitchen. Aside from a few foodstuffs, it was difficult to tell that someone actually lived there. Whitney rinsed out the coffee pot and looked in the cupboards for a filter. Finding none, he used a piece of paper towel as a filter and brewed himself a pot of coffee. He sat and stared out the kitchen window. The fresh mountain air had invigorated him, but there was still a lot he needed to think about. He finished the last swallow of coffee and fished a bottle of Scotch out of the liquor cabinet. He cracked a handful of ice from the tray in the freezer, put it in a glass and poured himself a hefty drink.

Whitney sat on the couch, hunched forward. *Damn, I hate everything about this fucking town.* He also hated everything about all of New Mexico and the entire Southwest. His job had become a pressure cooker. He was working a bunch of inexperienced cadets and not a one of them would ever progress beyond rookie.

Everything had been perfect under the previous chief of police, but when Suazo was appointed by the new Governor, a Democrat at that, the whole force was realigned. All the *Greasers* moved up a notch, much to Whitney's dismay. He was a dyed-in-the-wool bigot. The more he drank, the more he thought about all the changes that had made his life as a police officer more difficult. He had always loved his work. Now he hated to get up in the morning.

He walked out on the back deck and saw Ilfeld's car slowly pulling into the parking lot. Even from where he stood, he could hear the radio blaring. He watched as Ilfeld took his time unfastening his seat belt, turning the radio down and, from force of habit, smoothing his hair in the mirror.

"Late as usual," Whitney sneered. "Jerk's going to be late for his own funeral."

Ilfeld reminded him of Barney Fife, the bumbling deputy sheriff on the Andy Griffith Show. Even though they'd been friends and partners for years, Ilfeld still managed to annoy him regularly with his nonchalant Zen attitude about every aspect of his life. For a guy, he definitely had a Pollyanna approach that everything would be all right in the morning. This was one time where Whitney knew it wasn't going to be.

The doorbell rang twice. "Yeah, hold on a second," Whitney hollered. "Get your ass in here, Ilfeld," he said as he opened the door.

"Hey, Whitney, hello to you, too," Ilfeld smirked.

"Drink?" Whitney was already headed to the kitchen to replenish his.

"Yeah, sure. I'm off duty anyway," he plunked himself down on the easy chair facing Whitney and took a gulp of the drink. "So what's so darned important that it couldn't be handled on the phone? I was way the hell out in Española when you called."

Whitney glared at him. "If you haven't learned anything at all, you should know by now that cell phone conversations are the easiest mode of communication to track. A cell phone ping can practically draw a map of every place you've been in a given amount of time. If you had a listening device in your vehicle, your conversations could also be recorded. Doesn't take an idiot to know that."

"All right, so beyond the lesson in forensics, what else is new?" Ilfeld tugged at his collar.

Whitney was aware that that the heat was intense; he hadn't really bothered to crank up the air conditioning.

"I understand you were interviewed last week by Dr. Hodge, the forensic psychologist for the State."

"She was asking questions about Rose's death. Pretty cut and dried. Nice looking woman."

The furrows on Whitney's brow deepened. "And you're not at all concerned?"

"Concerned about what? Look, the case has been closed for almost ten years. Insurance money paid out a long time ago. Dr. Hodge said she was just tying up loose ends." He set his drink on the small table next to his chair.

Whitney took a long slow swallow of his drink and poured himself another. "You stupid idiot!" he fumed. "She's not tying up loose ends to close the case; she's tying up loose ends to reopen it."

"Oh, come on, Whitney. They don't have enough evidence to reopen the case. Everything was taken care of. There's no real file to speak of. No paper trail, not even a coroner's report. And on top of that, there's not even a coroner."

Whitney could see that his pacing was making Ilfeld nervous. "Think again," he said. "For your information, Chief Suazo found a bunch of old case files in one of the boxes our illustrious former Chief never bothered to pick up,"

Ilfeld's eyes almost popped. "You can't be serious. The guys disposed of anything they thought might be incriminating. Nobody would be able to make anything out of what was left."

"Apparently they didn't do a good enough job," Whitney said. "She's going to have to be taken care of. There's too much to lose. It's just a matter of time before she figures out the whole scenario."

"That's a little drastic, don't you think? Let me work it out. The statute of limitations runs out pretty soon. Maybe they won't reopen the case. Even if they do, I can tell them it was an accident. What good is it going to do to kill Hodge off?"

Ilfeld walked over to refill his own glass, not bothering to dilute it with ice. "She's too visible, for crying out loud, working for the Sheriff's Department and the State Police."

"We've got no choice," Whitney said. "Dr. Hodge is relentless. She's not going to back down. I don't know what else she has up her sleeve."

"She's just doing her job. Nobody else has been able to move this case forward. What makes you think she can? She got a magic wand or something?"

"In addition to being persistent, Jemimah Hodge is a brilliant forensic psychologist and an even better profiler. Every police department in the country would like to have her on staff. She just happens to like this God-forsaken desert. I know her. She's not going to drop it."

"I think you're opening up a hornet's nest here, Whit. Why don't you just leave it alone and let the dust settle?"

"Because she knows a hell of a lot more than she's letting on. And that *dust*, as you called it, is liable to settle on our butts. She could destroy both our careers." Whitney slurred and the ice in his drink jingled in his glass. "No telling what that old codger put her onto before he croaked. I'm sure you saw that in the newspaper."

"You mean that half-dead old guy they found out in the park? I saw his photo in the newspaper. He sure looked familiar. Who the heck was he?"

"None other than some old fart who used to be your wife's gardener. Apparently he was there on that day, practically standing in front of the window. How the hell we didn't see him is beyond me." Whitney was uncharacteristically buzzed as he sucked on the ice in his glass. "He says he saw it all come down—you choking her and all."

"Oh, shit. What am I going to do now? I might as well just give myself up and forget about it." Ilfeld was almost in tears, his New Age mantra of peace and harmony having sprouted wings and flown out the window. "I gotta call an attorney. No point in prolonging the misery."

Whitney was disgusted. "Can you hear yourself, Ilfeld? You sound like an idiot. Straighten up your act or you're going to blow everything right into the Sheriff's lap. Go home. Give me some time to work this out."

Ilfeld looked as though he was about to burst into tears. "What are you going to do?"

"Listen, I took care of that old man and I'm going to take care of her," Whitney declared.

Ilfeld looked stunned. Whitney could see he hadn't put two and two together and concluded that he had killed the old man. But his partner of fifteen years knew better than to confront him. Ilfeld stood up to leave.

"Don't be an asshole, Ilfeld," Whitney added. "You're not the only one that's going to be floating down shit creek if this whole thing hits the fan. Now get out of here. Let me think." Whitney all but pushed him out the door.

ᘓ

Ilfeld walked down the steps to the parking lot. He drove the ten miles from Whitney's place to the Fraternal Order of Police lodge out on Airport Road.

His friend's demeanor had unnerved him, but there wasn't a soul he could talk to about it, so he ordered himself a drink and settled in at the bar, intending to stay until closing time.

A collection envelope for a police officer injured while on duty circulated around the bar. He tossed in a twenty and passed it on to the next guy. The redhead sitting on the corner stool raised her glass to him and smiled.

Ilfeld asked the bartender what the lady was drinking and carried over a drink. Her long legs shifted on the barstool as he came closer.

"Kitty Legits. Long time no see," he smiled and pulled up a seat next to her.

Chapter Thirty-One

After a long work week, the weekend couldn't come soon enough for Jemimah. She planned to cozy up to a pitcher of margaritas and a good book. Maybe she'd watch a movie. Her assistant Katie had loaned her a chick flick, *How Stella Got Her Groove Back.*

Maybe it was time she got her own groove going. Jemimah laughed at her own analogy. The lead character in the movie dates a younger man. She couldn't even date someone her age. As she stepped out of the shower, she wrapped herself in a towel and dried her hair in front of the mirror.

"What a sad state of affairs, my dear," she said to the mirror. "Another Friday night, home alone." She giggled, knowing that if she really wanted to be somewhere else, she could be, but she preferred the solitude of her home in the hills near Cerrillos. She glanced at her dog sprawled out on the rug in front of the couch, "Guess you're my date for tonight, sweetie." Molly saw that there was no treat in Jemimah's hand so she grunted and drifted back to sleep.

Jemimah slipped into a pair of warm-ups and a sweatshirt, pulled her hair back and made her way to the kitchen. She gazed out the window at the subtle beginnings of what was gearing up to be a spectacular crimson sunset. Maybe she would go out on the patio and enjoy it for a while. She gave the margarita mix a thoughtful stir and poured some into a glass. She looked up as her dog jumped down from the couch, her ears perked up.

Jemimah turned as the front door flew open. She reached for her pistol, but then saw it was Captain Whitney. "Don't you knock anymore, Whitney?" She aimed her automatic pistol straight at him, unsure if his dramatic entrance was a joke or not.

"I could have sworn I emptied your gun the last time I was here," Whitney sneered.

"So I noticed. Just happened to have a spare clip," Jemimah lied. Shit. She knew Whitney was a crack shot. She was freaking out, struggling to stay in control. She wasn't about to let him know she was the least bit scared. She watched him closely. Jemimah had long suspected that beneath that smooth veneer was a criminal mind. His hand stayed firmly on his holster.

Jemimah tried to keep her voice light. She knew she wasn't a match for him. Although she always managed to hit the chest of the paper target at the firing range, she had never done it without flinching. She was no marksman. "Is this a joke, Whitney? Do you want a drink so bad that you have to kick my door in? Come on, sit down. You can share my pitcher of margaritas."

Whitney didn't respond. He stood and glared at her. She heard a soft click and found herself staring into the barrel of his weapon. She couldn't tell if she was more scared or surprised; the only thing she knew for sure was that there was nowhere to run.

She stalled for time. "All right, I give up. What's it going to take to get you to tell me what this is about? Am I under arrest or something? Show me the warrant." She placed her gun on the counter in a bold move.

She scoured the room for her dog. Molly sat in the corner chewing on a T-bone. She looked up, a sheepish look on her face, and skulked away, carrying the steak in her mouth. Whitney locked her in the laundry room. Molly didn't make a sound after that.

He sneered at Jemimah. She started to say something. "Shut up, Jem. This isn't a social visit."

"I gathered that from your dramatic entrance. I would have answered the door if you had bothered to knock," she said. "But now that you're here, maybe you'd like to sit down like a gentleman and fill me in on whatever seems to be going through your mind." She smiled warily.

"Don't get cute on me. In a few minutes you're going to be attacking me and my gun's going to go off. I'll have to file a report and of course I'll have to mention that we've been sleeping together for about six months now and you were starting to get jealous. You had too much to drink, came at me in a rage, end of story." Whitney blinked only once during his entire soliloquy.

Jemimah forced a smile. "That's pretty good, Whitney, but I haven't even had a chance to take a sip of my drink. Looks like the whole pitcher is going to waste, ice all melted and such."

"Not to worry, my sweet. We'll remedy that in short order. Sit down"' He shoved her on to a chair. Reaching into the liquor cabinet, he pulled out a bottle of Chivas Regal, one he'd brought as a gift the last time he paid her a visit. He poured two glasses and set them in front of Jemimah.

"Now drink."

"You're kidding me." Wide-eyed, Jemimah looked down at the glasses. "I don't drink straight liquor. I'm a margarita kind of girl, you know that. I'm open to sitting down with you and having a chilled glass filled with the contents of that pitcher."

"There's a first time for everything, Honey. After the first one, the rest will go down real easy. Now get to chug-a-lugging. Forget the margarita mix. Not hardly strong enough to accomplish my purpose."

Jemimah looked around the kitchen for anything she could use as a weapon. *Nothing.* "Hold on there, Whitney. I'm not sure I understand what's going on. Let's talk for a minute. At least give me an idea of what you're all in a tizzy about."

He was unsmiling, his face rigid. "You've gotten too goddamn close to this Ilfeld case. You're the only thing standing between me and my retirement pension, and I've worked pretty damned hard for that."

"All right. Well, at least let's sit down and talk about it. Nothing's come up in that case that's of any significance." She shifted her weight on the stool and looked him straight in the face.

"Don't pull that innocent act on me, Lady. I know damned well you've put two and two together and figured out how things might have gone down."

Whitney was raging, his face red and his fists clenched. Jemimah knew she'd better be careful. There wasn't going to be any cavalry off on the horizon riding to her rescue this time.

"Tell me everything, Jemimah. Let's see how good of an investigator you've become."

"Look, Whitney. I don't understand what you're talking about. You know I'm not a detective. I can assure you that whatever I say doesn't count for much. I just tell my superiors what I think, give them a little input, make a few notes in the file and then walk away. I can just as easily walk away from this one. No big deal. Case closed."

"You're lying through your teeth, Jemimah," he hissed. "I have a hunch you know a lot more than you're letting on. For one thing, you must have gotten a pretty comprehensive statement from that feeble old idiot."

Jemimah sat very still, trying to contain her astonishment. Where the hell could Whitney have gotten that information? She hadn't transferred Jerry Frazier's statement or any of her notes into the file yet. Everything was still in her briefcase. Detective Romero and Chief Suazo knew, but they wouldn't have discussed the matter with anyone, especially not Whitney.

"What are you talking about, Whitney? I've interviewed a few people, and nothing's come of it," she said. "Over a year ago you said there was no evidence to prove Rose Ilfeld's death was caused by anything other than an automobile accident on the way to the hospital."

"You're just trying to save your own neck. You know damned well you've got it in your mind that I might somehow be involved." His voice was just below a holler.

Jemimah couldn't keep from rambling. Her mind was numb. She replayed the events of the previous week in her head. How had she not noticed the change in Whitney's demeanor? Last week she'd finally realized the case had been mishandled from the get-go and so had scheduled a meeting with the brass early next week. She concluded Officer Ilfeld should have immediately been placed on administrative leave and precluded from participating in any phase of the investigation.

In addition, it was evident that his fellow officers had conveniently lost or misplaced key evidence, much of which would have proven without a doubt that Rose Ilfeld had been dead long before the accident.

She'd conducted a phone interview with the EMT on the scene, Roger Streeter, who she remembered from the Pueblo murder case. He'd been a forest ranger when she'd met him. She couldn't recall exactly how he'd been involved. He'd been friends with Rose and, as he'd loaded Ilfeld into the ambulance, had suspected that the man was pretending to be worse off than he actually was. He'd also wondered why Ilfeld had been spreading rumors that his wife had a chronic illness—rumors that Rose denied.

And then it came to her. *Oh my God.* Whitney was the second officer, the one Jerry Frazier said came to the Ilfeld house.

The house was silent except for the whirring sound of locusts on the willow tree outside the open kitchen window.

The granite counter top was empty except for the pitcher of margaritas, the bottle of Scotch and the two glasses. Jemimah's mind was racing. She hadn't a clue what to do. No way was she going to be able to sweet-talk Whitney into anything. From the look on his face, he was set on his course of action. He knew her pistol was still empty, so she had accomplished nothing with that bluff.

She glanced at the clock in the kitchen. It was seven-thirty. In the summertime, evenings in Santa Fe County stayed light until almost nine. A chill swept through her. It was happening again. The very thing she had discussed with Dr. Cade. And here it was. Staring her in the face.

The minutes ticked forward at a snail's pace. Had it really only been thirty minutes? It seemed like an hour. Jemimah felt momentarily displaced. This couldn't be happening. She could hear the rain beating against the windows, stop for a second and then resume. A cool mist blew through the open patio door.

Meanwhile Whitney's attention was entirely on her. His voice broke into her thoughts. "It's too quiet in here, Jemimah, darlin'," he drawled. "Mind if I play some music?"

She glared at him. "Suit yourself."

"How about a little John Fogerty? I know you get off on Creedence," he said, in a dripping, lascivious voice. He didn't wait for her response. " 'Proud Mary', hmmm. Maybe 'Jeremiah Was a Bullfrog.' You've got a nice selection of oldies here." Whitney clicked on the CD player and pumped the sound up. He laughed and broke into an impromptu dance. "Come on, Jem, lighten up a little. It's not the end of the world. Uh, oh yeah, I guess it is."

The song ended and another followed. Whitney reached over and lowered the volume.

If she somehow managed to survive, she'd never be listening to that CD again.

He poured her another drink. Jemimah could feel the

pounding in her head. The nausea moved up from her stomach to her throat. She wanted to vomit. She looked across at Whitney. What could she possibly have seen in him? Why had she never noticed how his lips pursed into a thin line when he spoke and how he rarely looked her straight in the eye? *How* had she fallen for the man's faux charisma?

"All right, Jemimah. Enough talking." He pushed yet another full glass of alcohol toward her.

"You bastard," she sneered.

"Now, now. Nice Mormon girls don't curse. Drink up, dearie. There's a lot more where that came from."

Jemimah stiffened as panic surged through her body. She was alone and she knew it. The tone of Whitney's voice had changed dramatically. He was indifferent to anything she said. She had no choice but to cooperate. She sank into the chair and reached for the glass.

Chapter Thirty-Three

Tim McCabe was headed toward the town of Galisteo, a few miles southeast of Cerrillos, to serve a warrant in a domestic dispute. Damn, he hated to be in the middle of petty arguments over who was going to stay in the house and who had to leave. Never knew when one of them idiots was going to lose it and go all Clint Eastwood on everyone around.

McCabe could have cut through the Crawford Ranch Road to get to Galisteo, but the county crews were grading the road. He headed toward Madrid, where he would cut across to Galisteo. It was a longer shortcut, but he enjoyed seeing the rock formations jutting into the turquoise sky. There was nothing else like it in the entire southwest.

Jemimah Hodge's small ranch was coming up on the road. He had promised Laura he would drop off the photos she'd developed from their last visit together. It wouldn't take but a few minutes, and besides, he had spent hardly any time with her lately. He liked Jemimah. She was like the daughter they never had. As he approached the turnoff to her ranch, he spotted the State Police cruiser in the driveway. His first thought was to continue on and catch her on the return trip. As he drove closer to the house he slowed down.

That's odd. The black and white is parked halfway into the grass, like someone got out in a hurry.

McCabe drove past the house and pulled off the road in front of the neighboring ranch.

Tim called Detective Romero.

"Rick, McCabe here. I'm on the outskirts of Cerrillos headed out to serve that warrant you left me. I'm outside Jemimah's place and I'm a little concerned."

"What's going on there, McCabe?" Romero said.

"Well, I might be a suspicious old worrywart, but it looks to me like Jemimah might have an unwelcome visitor. Whitney's cruiser is parked in her driveway, more on the grass than on the pavement."

"Well, you know he's been chasing her for over a year. Probably dropped by to shower her with flowers and candy." McCabe could hear that Romero was attempting to downplay his irritation.

"I don't think so, Amigo. My gut tells me something's wrong. A while back Jemimah told me how she felt about him, and there was nothing romantic about it. In fact, I think she was a little intimidated by his recent behavior. There'd be no reason for him to just stop by for a social visit. The way his cruiser's parked looks like he was in an awfully big hurry to see her. Driver's side door's halfway open. I think I should check it out. I was going to drop by on my way back, but maybe I should do it now."

"Dammit, McCabe. Now you've got me worried. She said she was sending me a memo about the case and when I got it I shoved it in my briefcase to read later. I'm just driving onto the Highway 14 exit. It will take me about fifteen minutes to get there. And if something is wrong, the siren would tip him off for sure. You're going to have to handle this yourself."

McCabe opened the glove compartment of the Hummer and retrieved a 9mm Smith and Wesson and the extra magazine, just in case. He slipped the gun into the waistband of his pants. He wasn't quite sure how he was going to proceed. All he knew was that Captain Whitney wasn't going to be easy to deal with. He was also concerned about what to say in case it turned out to be a social visit. It would be a big pain in the ass to have to explain walking in on two people in a compromising situation.

Romero retrieved Jemimah's memo, quickly scanning the page. He drove through the four-way stop in typical Santa Fe fashion, barely tapping the brake pedal while checking oncoming traffic. As he turned onto the exit, it was all he could do to keep from barreling ninety miles an hour down Highway 14. He ran the siren for the first five minutes and then switched to flashing lights only. He was working up a sweat merely from the tension.

I should have known Whitney was going to pull something like this. How could I have been so stupid! I should have assigned someone to watch her twenty-four/seven.

There was generally very little traffic on Highway 14 as the road wound into the hills of Cerrillos. Much of the daily traffic centered around the State Corrections Facility, the Sheriff's Complex across the road and the elementary school about five miles from Santa Fe. Romero lead-footed it down the road as he speed-dialed McCabe on his cell.

"Rick, where you at?" McCabe answered.

"A couple of minutes out just coming around the bend. I'm moving as fast as I can. Have you seen anything?" He slowed to a crawl as he reached the edge of Jemimah's property.

"Heard nothing, seen nothing," said McCabe.

"Okay, I'm pulling in across the street." Romero could see McCabe's Hummer in the next yard. "I see your vehicle. Where are you?"

"In the open barn facing the house. Go around the back. There's a door on the side."

"I'll find you."

CR

Romero scoured the area around him. It had been exactly fifteen minutes since McCabe called him. It was now past twilight. He stared at the front of the house, looking for any sign of life. Something didn't feel right. The security lights hadn't gone on and he knew they were on a timer. He walked along the coyote fence to the small iron gate on the side, following the path to the barn. He saw McCabe standing against the wall and motioned to him.

The rain started, quiet and gentle at first, followed by deafening bursts of thunder and lightning. This was going to be a gully washer. Cool, heavy drops pounded the roof and slid into the drains, filling the water barrels below in record time. The downpour drowned out any noise coming from anywhere around the property. Romero stood hunched over next to McCabe.

"I haven't seen any movement near the house, not even the dog," McCabe whispered. " 'Course, the dog knows Whitney, and so wouldn't consider him to be a threat, but she always flies out the doggie door anytime a vehicle approaches."

"We need to formulate a plan here, McCabe. Maybe they're just in there having a drink. Wouldn't be the first time." Romero recalled a particular instance when Whitney showed up at Jemimah's house long after dark, just about the time he was going to make his move on her. "No matter, I'm going to call in the SWAT team. I might be jumping the gun, but I can deal with that embarrassment if the time comes." He dialed Detective Chacon's number.

Romero had been to Jemimah's house on a few occasions. It took a while to get a sense of the floor plan, viewing it from the outside. They were a hundred feet or more from the sliding doors of the small patio leading into the west-facing kitchen. It was the only light reflecting from the side of the house and he assumed that's where Whitney was holding Jemimah, if indeed that's what was happening.

A chill ran through him as he pushed the potential possibilities to the side. Jem was strong. She was used to dealing with psychopathic behavior, but usually in the well-protected confines of an office. It had been a long time since he felt like praying, for anything, for anyone. Today was different. He looked toward Jemimah's driveway again. The thought crossed his mind that she might be dead. He didn't want to go there. Not now. Not when everything was falling into place. He was ready to tell her how he felt. No bullshit. Just *I love you*. He forced himself to focus.

"You okay?" McCabe's voice popped him back into the moment.

"Yeah, sure, just trying to figure out how come we're having another déjà vu moment here. Remember last year when that nutcase had Jemimah out on the Garden of the Gods threatening to throw her off the cliff? And here we are again. I wouldn't blame her for quitting her job and moving as far away from here as she can get."

"Yeah, she's been baptized by fire, twice," said McCabe. "Hey, you're pretty worried there, aren't you, Compadre?"

"I sure am. I just hope we can get her out of this mess. I'm trying not to think of what a disaster this could turn out to be in light of her suspicions about Whitney."

Chapter Thirty-Three

"What's the matter there, Honey, don't like my choice of drinks? Mine tastes just fine," purred Whitney. He wasn't concerned about having a few drinks, even while on duty. He'd always had a high tolerance for alcohol. The stronger the better.

"The drink is better than the company, Whitney," Jemimah barked back at him.

"I distinctly remember a time when you enjoyed my company, like most women do. You were putting away those margaritas like they were water," he continued to coo in a voice Jemimah found irritating.

"That was before I knew you were such a jerk," she said. Her spirits sank. She tried to convince herself everything would be all right. Whitney would come to his senses. Thoughts of dying wheedled their way into her head, filling her mind with a terror so raw she almost passed out. All her training seemed to be useless under these circumstances.

"Admit it, Jemimah. You had the hots for me and you know it." Whitney laughed, reached for the bottle and refilled her glass.

She had lost count of the number of drinks she had ingested and was beginning to feel woozy. "Don't flatter yourself, Whitney."

The severity of the situation was beginning to blur in her mind. It took an effort to maintain her composure. She could feel the tears burning in her eyes.

For God's sake, don't start crying. That's all I need.

Whitney stared at her. "Pretty quiet there, Lady. Contemplating your fate? I'll fill in the blanks for you. It will be dark pretty soon, and when you finish the next drink, we're going to mosey into that bedroom of yours and have ourselves a little consensual sex. I'm sure you're going to enjoy it just as much as I am."

"You won't get away with this," she said, her words beginning to slur.

"No use in fighting it, Honey. It's just part of the plan. I figure we might as well have a romp in your bed anyway, to make it more believable. Besides, I'm not passing up an opportunity to get you in the sack." Whitney poured himself another shot of Scotch, stirred it with his pinky, and took a long sip.

"You're sick, no question about it." Her voice was flat.

"Oh, isn't the good doctor going to try out her feminine wiles on her captor? What would Freud recommend right about now? Let me see ... we could have such great sex that I would change my mind and let you go." Whitney moved closer to her, brushing his lips against her cheek.

Jemimah flinched. "That's not going to happen." She could feel herself swaying as she attempted to stand.

"Let you in on something, Sweetheart. Detective Romero already thinks we've slept together and I haven't said anything to the contrary. The way you were throwing yourself at me last year didn't go unnoticed. After this, he'll have no doubt, won't have to wonder anymore. The autopsy, of course, will show that. It's standard practice now for the coroner to take a few swabs, if you get my drift," he chuckled.

Jemimah wished she could hit him with something, but she was hopelessly helpless. "You bastard."

"Drink up, Jemimah. Time's a wastin'."

Chapter Thirty-Four

A shiny black van with chrome rims and tinted windows slid to a stop on the highway in front of Jemimah's house. It edged forward at a slow pace and parked by a grove of cottonwoods. Four men in SWAT uniforms alighted from the vehicle and waited for their commander to give the order. Slowly moving forward, they crouched near the fence, weapons drawn.

As Chacon directed the SWAT team toward them, Romero glimpsed a State Police 4x4 cruiser pulling in behind the van. He watched the officer slip on a Kevlar vest over his uniform. Throwing his cap into the back seat of the vehicle, he reached for a U21 automatic.

Romero knew most of the officers but didn't recognize this one. He was standing too far away, his face blocked by the trees, and it was starting to get dark. Maybe he was from another district office. Romero radioed Detective Chacon, who had arrived a few minutes before the van.

"What's State Police doing out here? We didn't put in a call for them."

"Maybe SWAT did. Maybe he was in the area. Who the hell knows," said Chacon. "No time to be chasing anybody out of the sandbox. Should I tell him to lay back?"

"Nah, let it go. Maybe we can use another hand. Don't know how this whole thing's going to play out," Romero said.

"Okay, Boss, we're in position," said Chacon.

"Okay, Artie. Here's the plan." Romero explained the

layout of the house. "We believe Doctor Hodge is being held against her will by an officer suspected of murdering a key witness in a criminal case she's been profiling. We figure they're in the kitchen. That will be the second room north of the driveway. There's a small porch next to the French doors which open out to a patio and a fenced backyard. We'll be coming around the north side. Give me the go-ahead when you're ready. And, proceed with caution. The guy's a veteran cop. Probably heavily armed."

With his officers in place, Romero was about to give the ready signal, when the State Police officer jumped ahead of the others. Chacon tried to stop him. "What the hell is he doing?" Romero radioed Chacon. "Artie, what's going on?"

"The State cop took off up ahead of us, disregarding orders," McCabe said.

"Shit, he's armed to the hilt," Detective Chacon said. "Got enough weapons on him to fight a small army."

"Who the hell is he?" Romero said.

"I could read his tag as he was putting on his vest," McCabe said. "It said something like Hillfield. Didn't catch the first name. He said he was in the area and did we mind if he assisted. Said he works the anti-terrorist development team for the State Police."

"Officer Hillfield, if you're copying, stop where you are and let the team move into place," Romero hissed into the radio. His voice was almost a whisper. A pissed off whisper at that. He looked at McCabe. "Why is this guy taking the lead?"

"Maybe he knows Captain Whitney?" offered McCabe. "Anyway, he wasn't assigned a radio, so he's pretty much out of contact with us."

It took Romero a few seconds before it dawned on him. "Oh, shit. Ilfeld. *Not Hillfield.* That's the State Police officer in the cold case Jemimah was investigating. It's his wife who died in the accident. What the hell is he up to?"

Artie shrugged. "Not a damned thing we can do about it

now, Boss. He's already edging through the patio, from what I can tell," he said.

Romero motioned for McCabe to move in with him toward the driveway. The SWAT team went around the other side. There had been no sign of the dog and Romero hoped she wouldn't start barking now and blow their cover. Like mountain lions stalking their prey, the group moved silently toward the grassy area near the kitchen. Since he hadn't heard a sound, Romero figured Ilfeld was probably waiting for them to make their move. At least he hoped that's what was going on.

Then all hell broke loose.

Chapter Thirty-Five

"Hold it right there, Whitney," Ilfeld shouted as he stood in the entrance to the kitchen.

Whitney spun around, caught off guard. "Ilfeld, what the hell are you doing here?"

"Saving you from making another big mistake, my friend. Push away your weapon or I'll blow your head off," he yelled.

"You're not man enough, Ilfeld. If you leave now I won't be compelled to shoot you and include you in on a love triangle when I kill off Tootsie here," retorted Whitney.

"Come on, Whit. Drop the bullshit and give yourself up. There's no way you're going to get away with this," Ilfeld said.

Whitney hit the floor, his weapon drawn. Ilfeld fired one shot, straight through the heart.

The loud blast reverberated throughout the room. The SWAT team swarmed in as a wounded Ilfeld held on to the edge of the island. Whitney's shot had shattered his elbow. Ilfeld was stunned. He'd never intended to kill Whitney, who was more than a crack shot, the undisputed best on the force. Ilfeld knew the miss must have been deliberate, but right now the pain was excruciating and he was bleeding all over the place.

Romero and McCabe followed the SWAT team into the kitchen. He held his weapon tight as he scoured the room.

The only light on in the house was the hanging fixture over the granite island. It cast an eerie glow over Whitney's face as Detective Chacon pressed his fingers into his neck and felt for a pulse. "This guy's dead. Bullet right through the heart."

Jemimah was kneeling on the floor, half under the table. Romero whisked her up and carried her outside. Tears cascaded down her cheeks. She stifled a sob.

"I'm sorry," she whispered. Somewhere in the distance she could hear sirens wailing as they drew closer. She closed her eyes and wept silently.

Romero held her tight. "Nothing to be sorry about. You had no way of knowing this would happen. I'm just glad you weren't hurt." He reached in his pocket for a handkerchief and wiped her eyes. They walked to the bench in the patio, her hand clasped tightly in his. She couldn't talk. Words were stuck in her throat between sobs.

"I'm all right, Rick. Just a little shook up," she said.

"You've been through a God-awful experience, Jem. I'm not letting you out of my sight. Detective Chacon and McCabe can handle everything inside. You can give your statement when things calm down."

Romero sat with her as they waited for the ME's office to arrive and conduct their investigation.

Whitney's corpse was wheeled out of her kitchen in a body bag and transferred to the ME's van. A roll of yellow tape was carefully wound around the yard.

Jemimah was stunned. "Dammit, Rick. I should have realized Whitney was capable of something like this."

"Hey, take it easy on yourself. You're still in shock," he said gently. "For what it's worth, he fooled everyone."

"But I'm a psychologist. A criminal profiler. That's what I do for a living. How could I have missed the signs?"

Romero held her by the shoulders. He gazed straight into her eyes. "Jem, listen to me. Whitney was a hard-assed, seasoned police veteran with the mind of a psychotic. No telling what else he was into. Don't do this to yourself."

He sat with her until her breathing slowed and her hands stopped shaking. Jemimah knew she was still pretty drunk. She looked around for her dog.

"Oh, my God. Please don't let him have killed Molly," she said, clutching Romero's arm. He hurried into the house and found the dog in the locked laundry room where she had been since Whitney showed up. Molly yelped and tore through the kitchen and out the sliding door looking for Jemimah. Romero followed the dog into the yard. Whatever Whitney had slipped her must have worn off. She leapt into Jemimah's lap, showering her face with kisses.

"You're staying with me tonight, Jemimah," Romero said. "And don't give me any arguments." He gently kissed her cheek.

She looked up at him. There was no need to speak. It was over.

Chapter Thirty-Six

Outside the window, the birds were engaged in a chirping contest as the morning sun peeked through the curtains in the bedroom. Romero spread a light cotton blanket over Jemimah's shoulders. He had slept on the couch in the living room and had been awake since early morning.

The brew light on the coffee maker turned green as he set out a tray with two cups, cream and sugar. He poured the coffee and walked over and sat gently next to her on the bed.

"Wake up, sleeping beauty," he said.

She sat upright, "What time is it?"

"Nine o'clock. Cream and sugar?"

Jemimah threw the covers to the side. "Oh, Jeez. I have an appointment. I need to see the Sheriff this morning."

"No appointments. We're both off for the day. Sheriff Medrano assigned someone else to interrogate Ilfeld as soon as he's released from the hospital. There's not much we can do until that happens."

Jemimah stretched her arms over her head. "Wow, I haven't slept that well for months. You got some kind of magic potion in this room?"

"Nope. This is where I grew up. In a home with lots of love, lots of laughter, and a lot of mischief."

She looked at him with a shy grin. It was time to let the barriers down. This man was genuine. She knew he cared for her, but this wasn't the place or the time. She was going to play it by ear.

"All right, Detective, what's on the schedule for today, seeing we've been given a hall pass?"

"Thought we might take a drive up near the ski basin, change of scenery. Spend a little time breathing a different kind of air."

"Fresh air sounds great to me." The dog jumped on the bed and licked her face. "Molly's in full agreement."

cs

The runoff-filled Santa Fe River shuffled along, its waters creating small whirlpools as foamy ripples beat against the rocks. A group of teenagers on inner tubes struggled alongside the current, moving in every direction but forward, their joyous hollers echoing through the air. A lone fly fisherman stood on the banks, his movements as graceful as the breeze. Romero and Jemimah sat on the grass against an outcropping of dark rocks, looking toward Santa Fe Baldy off in the distance. The staggering mountain peaks were frosted with vanilla snow left over from a late spring storm. At this altitude, the snow hung around until midsummer. Jemimah leaned forward and placed her hand over his.

"Rick, I need to say something. I want to apologize."

Jemimah had a clean but enticing scent. Freshly scrubbed with soap and water. Not even a hint of perfume. He looked at her, about to respond with a question. She put her fingers over his lips.

"Let me finish. I've been such a bitch. My emotions have been incendiary, burning through any likelihood of developing a close relationship. It's taken me a while to work out the trauma caused by a series of events from my childhood. I've never said anything about this to anyone but my therapist," she said, her voice smaller than usual.

"Look, Jem. You don't have to explain. I understand."

"No, let me get this off my chest, please. Throughout all the time I've known you, Rick, I've served up small doses of hope, only to retract them in one swift movement. I can't even fathom how that must have appeared to you. I imagine you must have felt like a daisy—she likes me, she likes me not."

Romero laughed. "Pretty much."

"What I'm trying to say," she continued, "is that in recent months I've come to realize that no matter what may have happened in my childhood, it had nothing to do with you. For the first eighteen years of my life I lived in fear that I was going to be whisked up at any time by some old man, forced to marry him and have children. That would end any aspirations I might have to lead a normal life. Consequently, I was convinced that I would never be able to have a decent relationship. I proved it by getting married about a year after I left Utah, and the guy turned out to be a jerk. So since then I've pretty much kept everyone at bay, including you."

"Jem, none of that matters now. You need to put all that behind you," he said gently.

"Ah," she teased. "That sounds like the voice of psychoanalysis speaking. Has the good detective been seeing a shrink?"

"Guilty," he said. "And it seems to have started taking hold. I've learned a lot about myself, things I was never willing to face. I'm not perfect, Jemimah, but I'd be willing to give it a go if you are."

"Does this mean that you're asking me on a date?" she grinned.

"Yes, it does. I'd like to ask you out on lots of dates," he laughed. "But I'd settle for one."

"One it is, then," she said.

"Pick you up at eight?"

"Uh, sure," she giggled. "What night?"

"Friday. You know that's official date night."

"Considering the Friday night I just experienced, let's make that Saturday," she said.

A determined whirlwind pirouetted in front of them. Jemimah took the scarf from her neck and tied it around her hair. He noticed how her golden hair sparkled in the sunlight. She subconsciously reached up and pushed a few loose strands over her ear.

Romero put out his hand and pulled her upright. "Let's find another spot," he said. "The sun seems to have hidden under a cloud." He paused, then said, "Jemimah, as a psychologist, perhaps you can explain something. It has been nearly ten years since Whitney helped Ilfeld cover up his wife's death. If he really was a psychopath, how was he able to keep it under wraps for so long? Do you suppose there are other killings he perpetrated that we don't know about?"

Jemimah shrugged, then shook her head. "Ilfeld saw him skimming from drug money, we know that. That may have been the full extent of his crimes up till that point. By helping Ilfeld get away with killing his wife, he was doing his buddy a favor and keeping him quiet at the same time. He thought of himself as invincible, so he probably didn't consider it much of a risk. And remember that he didn't kill Rose, so he hadn't committed murder at that point. But clearly, money was a major motivator. And keeping his reputation intact. The thought of losing on both accounts was enough to put him over the edge. Killing a lesser being who was going to die anyway—a poor, sick old man—probably didn't seem like a major deal to him. He'd tried to kill you, but you'd lived, so that didn't count. You were a rival in so many ways, so he felt justified. In my case as well … I'm a woman, and he obviously had no respect for women in general. Especially one who dared to challenge his authority. Over the years he slipped, little by little, into dangerous territory psychologically, convincing himself that he was justified and then not caring anymore. A wild animal kills when it's cornered or hungry. Even a lion is perfectly safe when it's well fed and unthreatened."

"Do you think Ilfeld killed his wife for the insurance money?"

"He did spread those rumors that she had Leukemia. Although he claims that he made up the illness to explain his wife's absence on social occasions. Says she'd found out he was stepping out on her and didn't want to have to put on a show in public that everything was fine. He claims he never meant to kill her, and I guess I believe him. After all, if you want to invent an illness, you can do better than chronic Leukemia, which people can live with for years. Not to mention the fact that an autopsy would reveal that she was healthy. He didn't think that part through. All that jibes with his accidental death claims."

They walked a well-worn path next to the river bank. He pointed to a small outcropping of rocks on the side of a hill where they could sit undisturbed by everything but the sounds of nature. A stray dog nearby entertained the thought of coming toward them. The hair on Molly's back bristled and she barked out a warning. She, too, was in the mood for some peace and quiet.

They rode in silence on the drive back to Santa Fe. A day in the mountains outside of Santa Fe had proven far more therapeutic for them both than any psychologist's couch.

Chapter Thirty-Seven

Carlos hadn't been around for a few days and that was fine with Romero. As long as he wasn't back in jail. Romero figured he was probably still hanging around Sandra like a dog in heat.

Today was going to be a busy one for Romero. He was scheduled for a television interview about Whitney's involvement in the Rose Ilfeld case, and to attend Don Ilfeld's arraignment for involuntary manslaughter. By the time he arrived at his office, there was a stack of messages on his desk.

The phone rang and he swiveled his chair to answer it. The caller ID flashed his brother's name and number.

"Carlos, what's up? I've only got a minute," he said, flipping through the sheaf of messages. He crumpled a few and tossed them into the trash.

"I'm in trouble, Rick. Come get me," Carlos said.

"Where are you?" Romero said.

Carlos mumbled something unintelligible.

"Stay right there. It'll take me about thirty minutes. Don't move." Romero grabbed his keys and headed toward the door.

"Hey, hey, hey," Clarissa shouted after him. "You have a meeting in twenty minutes."

"Cancel it. Make up an excuse. No, better still, call Detective Chacon and let him handle it," he said. "He likes bright lights and cameras."

He heard Clarissa say "Never a dull moment around

here" before he pulled out of the driveway, burning a layer of rubber on the asphalt.

Romero sped down the interstate to the Glorieta turnoff and wound his way up the one-lane road to the village of Pecos. He took the turn leading to the fish hatchery and then drove into the parking lot of the Benedictine Monastery. A rotund monk with a tonsured head was standing in front of the chapel, next to a life-sized statue of Saint Benedict. A man in his sixties, he was dressed in a hooded long black tunic typical of the habit of his Order.

"I'm Brother Timothy. Are you Detective Romero?" He reached out to shake Romero's hand.

"Yes, I am, Brother. What's going on with Carlos; where is he?" He was oblivious to the tranquility of the monastery as his insides churned.

"He's inside, drying off," Brother Timothy said softly.

"What happened to him; is he all right?" Romero said, as Brother Timothy led him down a long porch.

"It's probably better he explain, my Son."

He pushed the door open and motioned for Romero to enter. The room was sparingly furnished with only a bed and a small table. A wooden crucifix and lit votive candle sat on the table next to a small bouquet of wildflowers. Two framed religious prints hung on the wall. It was the picture of serenity. Carlos sat on the edge of the bed, slumped forward, his head leaning heavily on his hands.

"Are you okay, Carlos?" Romero said.

"Yeah, I guess," he looked sheepishly at Romero. His eyes were red and his clothes were damp and wrinkled. There was no doubt in Romero's mind that his brother had probably tied on a good one. The smell of sweat and liquor seeped through his pores.

"You look like hell. Where's your car?" Romero said.

"Last I remember it was buried in about three feet of water, somewhere around here," Carlos said.

"Where? Monastery Lake's the only water around here," Romero said.

"That would be it." Carlos started to say something else and then choked back a sob. "I cared about her, Rick. I really did."

"Who? Sandra?" Romero said.

"She dumped me. She friggin' dumped me. Said she was going back to San Francisco," his jaw clenched. "She didn't want to see me anymore. I wasn't good enough for her."

"Let's get out of here, Carlos. You can tell me about it on the way home. We need to get you cleaned up." He looked at Brother Timothy, standing in the doorway. "Thank you," Romero said.

Romero saw Carlos start to protest then think better of it. It would take several days for the tow truck to come for his vehicle. He must have known, drunk or not, that three feet of water wasn't enough to drown in. Romero assured Brother Timothy he would arrange for the tow truck and thanked him again for looking after his brother.

Carlos leaned forward in the passenger seat, his arms resting on the dashboard, his head bent forward.

"Buckle up," said Romero.

It took Carlos a few minutes to snap on the seat belt. His coordination was still soaked in the aftereffects of the alcohol.

"I shoulda never gotten involved with that woman," Carlos said.

"Cool down, Carlos. Just be thankful you weren't hurt," Romero said.

"I wasn't going to kill myself, if that's what you're thinking," Carlos explained in an indignant tone. "I was just so damned angry that I drove up here to think things out. I guess I shouldn't have finished off the bottle, either, but I couldn't help myself. The more I thought about her, the madder I got, and the more I drank. And, yeah, I know the terms of my probation prohibit drinking, so go ahead and turn me in."

"So how did your car end up in the lake?" Romero said, ignoring his remark.

"I started to back up and instead of hitting the brakes I hit the gas. Before I knew it I was up to my ears in water. Brother Timothy heard me hollering, he tossed me a rope and pulled me out."

Romero wanted to laugh but his brother had such a pathetic look on his face. "Don't worry about it, Carlos. You'll have your wheels back in a few days. I'll get one of the boys from the County to come out here and get it. It's a new car, so the warranty might cover some of the water damage."

Romero knew what it was like to be on the receiving end of a split. Although Carlos had only been dating Sandra for a short time, he didn't find it wise to minimize the impact of the breakup. When his own wife divorced him ten years ago, Romero had remained in a drunken stupor for weeks before finally checking into rehab.

Chapter Thirty-Eight

The aroma of Mexican food wafted out into the parking lot of La Choza Restaurant, a tiny Mexican food eatery tucked into the southernmost corner of the Railyard District off Guadalupe Street. Owned by the same family who operated The Shed, a trendier restaurant in the heart of Santa Fe, La Choza was the more casual of the two establishments. The old converted adobe house had uneven white plastered walls, wooden beams and low ceilings, with a kiva fireplace in one corner of the main dining room. A large picture window looked out toward the busy construction site of the new Railyard Center. Every hour or so the Railrunner commuter train zipped by on the tracks twenty feet from the parking lot.

As she stood with Romero at the hostess desk waiting to be seated, Jemimah could see their reflection in the mirror behind the register. They made a striking couple, even if she thought so herself. She was wearing a cranberry red knit top and black jeans. High-heeled boots made her appear almost as tall as he was. Romero was out of the dress suit required on the job and wore a long-sleeved blue cotton pullover and a pair of Levis. His alligator boots were far more comfortable than the black oxfords he wore to work each day.

She knew Romero's schedule of late hadn't allowed time for regular meals. He seemed jumpy. Maybe he was just hungry or jazzed up on caffeine. After a ten minute wait, the hostess seated them in a corner booth. This was their first official date and she was flattered by the way he couldn't seem to stop looking at her.

Jemimah lowered her long eyelashes. "Stop, already; you're embarrassing me," she laughed.

"Must be the full moon," he said, adding, "You look beautiful."

☙

Every sappy cliché Romero could think ran amok through his mind.

Where have you been all my life? You're the kind of girl a guy wouldn't mind bringing home to Momma. Whoa! Did you see my heart somewhere? I think I just lost it.

He needed for Jemimah to see his serious side, not the person most everyone else perceived him to be as a law officer. He inhaled deeply, grateful when the waitress handed them each a menu. As she droned on about the specials of the night, he told himself, *Take a hike, macho man.*

They dipped warm blue corn tortilla chips into the small bowl of fiery red salsa and engaged in small talk about the Railyard area until the waitress brought their meal. He ate a forkful of an enchilada and the hot red chili sauce burned right through his tongue and cleared his sinuses.

It was good pain, though, familiar since childhood at Grandma Benita's kitchen table, where everyone gathered for Sunday dinner. Red chili enchiladas smothered with onions and cheese, a pot of beans and tortillas. And on cold winter days, a big pot of posole and green chili stew. Romero spent much of his adult life trying to recreate those meals. This restaurant was right on target. He laughed inwardly as he thought perhaps he should have married a nice Spanish girl who could cook the traditional meals he loved. He doubted there were any women like that left. The ones he met were pursuing careers, not interested in archaic callings such as homemaking. Who was he kidding? He'd go nuts if he had a wife who stayed home all day and cooked. Then he'd have to spend a lot of time rehashing his day when he got home. *Borrrring!*

He ate another forkful of food and washed it down with a swallow of Corona, knowing he'd better keep these thoughts to himself. His relationship with Jemimah was moving forward nicely and he didn't want to say anything that might topple the apple cart.

"A little bit of an appetite there, soldier," she said. She laughed and shook her head. "It has taken me about a year to get used to the stinging burn of green chili on my tongue," she admitted. "I finally realized that if I was going to dine out in any of the local eateries here in Santa Fe, red or green chili was probably going to be on the menu." She spooned a hefty portion of chicken, guacamole and sour cream onto a tortilla and topped it with an extra helping of salsa.

"We both seemed to have worked up a hunger," he said, laughing.

After dinner they got up to dance. Fortunately for him the band was playing an old George Jones song, "I Always Get Lucky With You." Slow dancing was just his speed. He could feel her breath on his shoulder as they danced. The subtle smell of her perfume remained long after they returned to the table. He reached for her hand.

"Let's get out of here," he whispered.

"Lead the way," she whispered back.

They walked out into the parking lot. It felt as though all the barriers between them had been dissolved in the preceding week. She leaned against the car while he opened the passenger door, still holding on to her hand. "I'm sorry, Jem. I've been waiting a long time to do this."

She looked up at him, eyes wide with surprise. He bent forward and kissed her, gently at first. Her arms wrapped around his neck. He was surprised by her surrender. She allowed herself to fall completely into his arms, as though she'd trust him with her life. Which she had, of course. In that moment he felt certain that she returned his feelings.

Later that night he smiled at her and wiped his forehead, laughing.

"Jeez, Jem. I didn't think that position was even possible."

"Come here, you," she smiled seductively.

Chapter Thirty-Nine

Early on the evening of September 10th, Rick Romero and Jemimah Hodge walked hand in hand up Washington Avenue in Santa Fe. Along with a throng of over thirty thousand people, residents and tourists alike, they were headed up the hill to Fort Marcy Park for the annual burning of *Zozobra*, a fifty foot marionette-like figure whose alias was Old Man Gloom.

As the annual kickoff event for the annual Santa Fe Fiestas, a white-clad figure is constructed from the bottom up of wood planks and chicken wire, covered with cloth, and stuffed with five hundred pounds of shredded paper and firecrackers. The giant puppet is enormous, jutting into the cloud-filled sky, waiting for darkness. The stuffing inside the figure is meant to represent all the problems and frustrations experienced by everyone in attendance, and the entire community at large.

The couple sat on the grass, holding hands and looking up at the massive figure in childlike awe. The band began to play as the sky darkened. Old Man Gloom moaned and groaned, his long arms flailing as his booming voice echoed throughout the valley.

His red eyes outlined with black paper lashes rolled and his head bobbled from side to side. A dozen fire dancers whirled around the base of the figure, carrying flaming torches as they teased and threatened to light the fires that would send the colossal giant up in flames. Finally, the clothing of the figure started to burn, and within moments the blaze began moving slowly up to the giant puppet's head, engulfing his entire being in red and yellow flames. Loud and pathetic groaning could be heard throughout the city and beyond as Zozobra headed for his demise. When the flames reached his chest, the firecrackers inside exploded. Below him the fireworks display ignited and burst into a brilliant light show. The crowd shouted in tandem, "Burn him, Burn him!" The chanting continued as the figure burned to the ground. A loud cheer resounded as everyone jumped to their feet.

Jemimah laughed as Romero lit a match to a small pile of firecrackers and paper notes in front of them.

"This is all the crap we've gone through in the past year. Good riddance," he said, as it crackled and sputtered, the flame dying out quickly.

She reached over to embrace him. They stood up and followed the crowd toward the Plaza. The celebration had indeed begun. With any luck, the bad guys would take a break for the weekend.

Marie Romero Cash was born in Santa Fe, New Mexico, to a family that would eventually number seven children, and has lived there most of her life. After graduating from Santa Fe High School, she took a job as a legal secretary, a field that would provide a lifetime of employment. But then, in her mid-thirties, she discovered the traditional arts of northern New Mexico. After twenty years of creating award-winning art, she began to write about it, but decided she needed a higher education to do so. At fifty she enrolled in college and, five years later, graduated with a degree in Southwest Studies. In 1998, she received the prestigious Javits Fellowship to pursue her education. Since then Marie has written several books about the art and culture of the southwest, including a memoir about growing up in Santa Fe.

Deadly Deception is the sequel to *Shadows among the Ruins*, Cash's first novel. Coming soon: *Treasure among the Shadows*, the next book in the Jemimah Hodge Mystery Series.

You can find Marie on the Web at;
MarieRomeroCash.camelpress.com.

CPSIA information can be obtained
at www.ICGtesting.com
Printed in the USA
FSOW01n1211080116
15586FS